Heart Sun waited anxiously for the crow to appear

In his vision, the crow was as large as a condor. A terrifying caw sounded from its throat, a sound so piercing that the sun had split in half, as if in fear of the noise. Darkness then covered the land.

And the warrior who was to come and deliver Heart Sun's people stepped out of the darkness. The warrior in his dreams came in black, but his skin was clearly white. There was great pain on his face. Pain unlike any Heart Sun had ever seen, could ever imagine a man enduring without going insane.

And in the warrior's eyes was Death.

MACK BOLAN

The Executioner

DON PENDLETON's EXECUTIONER

MACK BOLAN

Blood and Thunder

A GOLD EAGLE BOOK FROM
W🌐RLDWIDE

TORONTO • NEW YORK • LONDON • PARIS
AMSTERDAM • STOCKHOLM • HAMBURG
ATHENS • MILAN • TOKYO • SYDNEY

First edition November 1986

ISBN 0-373-61095-5

Special thanks and acknowledgment to
Dan Schmidt for his contributions to this work.

Printed in Canada

Even God cannot change the past.

—Aristotle, *Nicomachean Ethics*, VI.2.1139b

"I wouldn't change a goddamned thing."

—Mack Bolan, at his trial.
On being asked how, given
the chance, he would relive
his life.

THE
MACK BOLAN
LEGEND

Nothing less than a war could have fashioned the destiny of the man called Mack Bolan. Bolan earned the Executioner title in the jungle hellgrounds of Vietnam, for his skills as a crack sniper in pursuit of the enemy.

But this supreme soldier also wore another name—Sergeant Mercy. He was so tagged because of the compassion he showed to wounded comrades-in-arms and Vietnamese civilians.

Mack Bolan's second tour of duty ended prematurely when he was given emergency leave to return home and bury his family. Bolan made his peace at his parents' and sister's gravesite. Then he declared war on the evil force that had snatched his loved ones. The Mafia.

In a fiery one-man assault, he confronted the Mob head-on, carrying a cleansing flame to the urban menace. And when the battle smoke cleared, a solitary figure walked away alive.

He continued his lone-wolf struggle, and soon a hope of victory began to appear. But Mack Bolan had broken society's every rule. That same society started gunning for this elusive warrior—to no avail.

So Bolan was offered amnesty to work within the system against international terrorism. This time, as an official employee of Uncle Sam, Bolan wore yet another handle: Colonel John Phoenix. With government sanction now, and a command center at Stony Man Farm in Virginia's Blue Ridge Mountains, he and his new allies—Able Team and Phoenix Force—waged relentless war on a new adversary: the KGB and all it stood for.

Until the inevitable occurred. Bolan's one true love, the brilliant and beautiful April Rose, died at the hands of the Soviet terror machine.

Embittered and utterly saddened by this feral deed, Bolan broke the shackles of Establishment authority.

Now the big justice fighter is once more free to haunt the treacherous alleys of the shadow world.

PROLOGUE

Fire and blood.

These were the elements in which a young marksman had been baptized in the war-torn jungles of Vietnam. To Mack Bolan, those days now seem an eternity ago. Since then he has walked alone on one long journey through hell. A personal crusade against the Mafia. A presidentially sanctioned war against the KGB and terrorists the globe over.

He was on his own again, the way he wanted it. A lone wolf with no one to turn to, nowhere to run, except firepower first into the killzones of his choosing. But the hell-miles had taken a heavy toll on the man.

Pain showed stark on his granite-hard face and deep in his ice-blue eyes, carving out a tombstone visage of a warrior who was of, but seemingly beyond, death. As if the hand of death couldn't touch him.

It hadn't yet.

But how long could he keep denying the end in his war of containment against the cannibals?

Bolan felt a pain, like a knife slicing through his guts, as he recalled the suffering and death of the brave soldiers and good men he had seen fall during his crusade.

The deaths of his parents and sister in Pittsfield.

The shell that was Aaron "The Bear" Kurtzman, crippled during the attack on Stony Man Farm.

The bullet intended for Bolan that instead claimed the life of April Rose.

Bolan's mind sifted through the black memories of shattered love and hope, the rubble of dead dreams. It wasn't pity or self-pity he experienced. It was the acceptance of certain harsh realities by a warrior who had tasted the powers of life and death. And life, Bolan knew, was a harsh reality. Evil never slept.

Now, as Bolan crossed the Arizona border and drove his four-wheel-drive GMC Jimmy into New Mexico, he wondered just where the blood journey would finally end.

Does a man create his own path to destiny, or is fate something handed out by forces beyond a man's control and reason? Certainly, Bolan had seen, the weak of body, those without the courage to face circumstances head-on, were puppets for those who wanted to pull the strings.

And savage man not only jerked those strings, but often severed them.

Bolan wished to forget for a while these thoughts that troubled him. He needed some R and R badly. But the ride from his and Johnny's San Diego strongbase had been a long and lonely run. The hours had seemed endless, allowed Bolan to sink into a state of deep reflection. The constant rush of wind through the cab had mesmerized him, put him in touch with thoughts and feelings that were always there, but only surfaced during periods of isolation away from the hellzones.

Was his war of containment against the ravagers of life an exercise in futility? Had anything changed? And just who really gave a damn?

Mack Bolan gave a damn. But he also realized one very important thing about his war. He couldn't change the heart of animal man. Pain, suffering and inevitable death were the only realities that could make a man see more than just his own immediate existence and needs. Time and again, Bolan had seen the human predators' destructive nature.

Too many damned times.

Enough times to leave Mack Samuel Bolan feeling as if a grappling hook had lodged in his flesh, could, at any time, tear open his chest, rip through his heart right down into the pit of his guts.

And what about the really innocent victims of the world? Those who couldn't defend themselves, born into battle-scarred environments they didn't create. The unwanted, abandoned at birth, or cut out of a mother's womb and thrown away like so much garbage. Didn't they matter to anyone?

Yeah, they should have mattered the most.

There were many ways, Bolan had seen, to kill besides outright murder by gun, hand or knife. Evil didn't always attack face-to-face. In fact, its very cowardice was its greatest weapon. A man could kill another by his tongue. A man's heart could be his deadliest weapon. And his own destruction.

Damn! He just wanted to forget. For a week. A day even.

But Bolan recalled his last phone conversation with Hal Brognola.

"I know you could use some R and R in the worst way, Striker," the big Fed had told him. "By God, nobody deserves it more than you do. But I've got an urgent situation. One that might have national and world-shattering impact if it's what intelligence thinks it might be."

Bolan recalled the weary sigh he had expelled. The memory sounded like the rattle of tumbleweed in his ears. Sure, he could have used the rest. But there was no such thing as rest and recreation in a world where the savages and warmongers never let up in their hunger to devour.

"Lay it on me, Hal. I'll decide. If it's that urgent, you know I'll hang it out there."

"John Engels. Name ring any bells?"

"Damn right the name clicks. Paramilitary operative for the Company. Military adviser in Vietnam. A mercenary who sells his services to the highest bidder. He thought he could take care of the Communist-backed guerrillas in Central America by himself. After he formed his own hit squad and wiped out a few villages, the Company dismissed him."

"And later put out a liquidation mandate, but dropped it. You've done your homework."

"It's all there in the computers at Stony Man."

"Well," Brognola had gone on, "Engels just disappeared after the Company fiasco in Central America. But intel believes he's surfaced. And he's more than just a common gun-for-hire, Striker. Intelligence believes that Engels and another renegade, one Harold Katterhagen, smuggled large amounts of opium out of Thailand near the end of the war.

"The Company, as usual, claimed never to have had any knowledge about black market action. But we both know the spooks had their hands in heroin and arms. Yeah, a dirty war. A lot of tricks were pulled by our guys just to keep pace with the Cong. Spooks, acting either on their own or with Company sanction, used heroin to help finance that war, recruit ARVN troops. So the Engels drug connection is a very real possibility, particularly in light of certain recent events."

"Like what?"

"Engels must have kept his Thailand pipeline open. Feds working on the case over the past two years believe these renegades might be financing international terrorism with heavy firepower. Bazookas, the best in subguns, even howitzers. Chief purchasing agents are the PLO and South African right-wing death squads, they believe. Engels and his gang sell the opium to major druglords right here in the States, buy out massive shipments of arms on the black market, then jack the prices up and turn around and sell the stuff."

"Intel got all this?"

"No. But a couple of big-shot pushers were picked up by Feds in Miami. The punks squawked, gave a

description of Engels, but no name. They were found
two days later in their cells with bullets in their heads.
They'd been making regular flights out to New Mexico. You were right, by implying that Engels is little
more than a gangster.''

"I wasn't implying, Hal. I was stating cold fact. But
anyone who peddles murder and sabotage right under
our noses is definitely very dangerous.''

"Engels has to be found and stopped, Striker. This
mission is all-out search and destroy.''

"Okay. But search where? Destroy what?''

"Every Fed working this case who uncovered some
lead turned up dead," Brognola had said. "They were
working under deep cover in New Mexico and Arizona at the time. They must've gotten too close to the
hardsite, seen something. These renegades have to be
organized like a crack paramilitary unit to have survived this long.''

"Or they've bought someone out.''

"That's a very real possibility, too. When our guys
were found, they'd been dumped in roadside ditches.
These animals must have made them lie facedown in
the dirt. Then blew their heads off. I'm talking about
young guys, looking to crack their first big case. Guys
with wives and children.''

Bolan remembered then the white-hot fury that had
boiled in his guts when Brognola told him that. The
fire just raged inside, became all-consuming when he
thought about the Feds rounded up and slaughtered
like sick cattle. Engels had gotten away with murder
before in Central America, and he was running wild

again. The savage was a traitor to his country, a butcher of men.

Mack Bolan would be damned if he didn't do something to strike these bastards dead.

"There's a strip of desert highway in northeast New Mexico where most of the bodies have been found," Brognola had said. "You could start there. Will you look into it, Mack?"

"No, Hal," the big warrior had told the Fed. "I'll do more than just look into it."

Bolan's mind returned to the present. He was there now, on that highway of death. Wind screamed in his ears. He adjusted his sunglasses.

Beneath a canvas tarp in the back of his Jimmy rested a .444 Marlin with infrared scope, the Beretta 93-R, a garrote and a 20-shot mini-Uzi known as "Little Lightning." Bolan's blue sport coat hid Big Thunder, riding in quick-draw leather on his hip.

The lone wolf was loaded down for war.

Search and destroy.

Full scale.

He would hunt the traitors down, and terminate them with no questions asked. He would find them, even if that meant chasing them straight into hell.

Suddenly, Bolan saw a vehicle loom up in his side-view mirror. He cursed himself for letting his thoughts wander for so long. Warning alarms sounded in his brain.

The black jeep blew by Bolan in the northbound lane. He counted four heads, but it was the bulk of something metallic in the back of the jeep that alerted him to danger.

An instant later, Bolan saw lights flashing in the shimmying side glass, then a highway patrol car shot past him like a rocket. Dust roiled up from the road-side ditch in the slipstream.

But the chase didn't last long.

The jeep swung off the highway, moved down a dirt road. Clouds of thick brown dust swept over the rig, obscuring it as it slewed to a halt.

One hundred yards down the empty, sun-baked highway and closing down fast, Bolan watched as the patrol car turned off the highway, stopped. The trooper shoved open his door.

The back flap of the renegade dropped. Sunlight glinted off the barrel of an M-249 SAW as the gunner poked the nose through the opening.

Radio mike in hand, the trooper froze as his feet touched dirt.

But the officer never made that call for backup.

Bolan gritted his teeth. He hit the gas, snaking Big Thunder from out of his hip holster.

But he knew he was too late to save the patrolman.

A lightning flash of hot lead dropped the trooper where he stood.

Bolan had just found the first link in the traitor chain.

1

Bolan knew he would be the gunner's next target. Murderers wanted no witnesses.

With panther-quick reflexes, Bolan threw the wheel hard left, slammed on the brakes. A hail of 5.56 x 45 mm tumblers swarmed over his 4x4. He felt the rig shudder on its wheels as it began a long sideways skid. Bolan ducked beneath the wheel as slugs drilled through the windshield, shattered safety glass, ripped open upholstery. Glass cubes razored through the cab, and he felt the fragments sting his face. Big Thunder came up in his fist to return fire. He kicked open his door.

But for some reason the driver of the assault jeep ground the clutch, and the vehicle shot away toward rugged desert country.

The mighty .44 AutoMag thundered three times, cannoned a lightning trio of rounds that blew three tires on the fleeing jeep. The driver momentarily lost control and the rig climbed a boulder, then hammered down on limp rubber.

His heart pounding in his ears, adrenaline burning like wildfire through his veins, Bolan ran up to the fallen trooper.

The patrolman was facedown in a growing pool of blood and a bed of broken glass, his legs kicking out in spasms.

Bolan looked up and glimpsed the jeep as it recovered, then sped recklessly across the sagebrush- and boulder-studded plain.

The stainless steel .44 by his side, the big, grim-faced warrior gently rolled the trooper over. Bolan bit back a curse.

Blood bubbled over the man's lips. The trooper stared up at Bolan, his eyes glazed over by pain, delirium. He struggled to part crimson-slick lips. "M-mister..."

"Easy, soldier. Did you radio for backup?"

"No...chance..."

Bolan knew the man wouldn't last long. A line of slugs had stitched him across his stomach. Blood pumped freely from his open guts as if it was being suctioned out.

Gut-shot and dying.

"Get...those bastards...."

"Hang in there, soldier. I'm coming back for you."

Holstering the silver hand cannon, Bolan sprinted back toward his Jimmy.

FLATTENED TREAD jounced over rock, slung the gunner against the side of the jeep. "Who the hell is that guy?" he shouted, staring over the M-249 SAW at the vehicle in pursuit, which spit up a spool of dust behind it.

"Just shut up, Kiley," the driver roared, his face flushed with fear and fury. "I'll slow down, draw him in. This time, you make sure you nail that bastard."

A massive man, with a crewcut that emphasized his bullet-shaped head, squeezed into the opening beside Kiley, swung up his Swedish M-45 subgun. "Looks like I'd better help you out there, Petie," he rasped, as dust swirled around his face. "Since you couldn't drop our hero boy before."

Pete Kiley bared his teeth. A snarl cut the lines in his ferret features. He knew damn well he should've nailed the son of a bitch in the first place. "Hell, it wasn't my fault that Stemmons panicked and hit the gas," he told Bullet Head, as he screwed his head around toward the driver. "You stayed put another coupla seconds, I'd have dropped him just like that Smoky."

"We don't have time to be dickin' around out here," Stemmons growled. "Just do it right this time."

"Yeah, sure," Kiley muttered. "We don't call ourselves the Apocalypse Brigade for nothin'."

But Kiley's boast sounded hollow, his voice swept away by wind blasting through the cab.

BOLAN CUT THE GAP to a hundred feet in less than a minute. He saw the hardware the scum leveled at him from the jeep's open back. A heartbeat, and Bolan peeled away from the trail of dust, the line of fire. He knew they were baiting him, trying to suck him into their death trap.

The uneven desert floor, threatening to kick Bolan out of his seat, jarred him to the bone. Creosote bushes and sagebrush flew up behind the rampaging rig. Bolan redlined the Jimmy. A jackrabbit streaked across his path like a missile, as the 4x4 plowed through cactus.

The Squad Automatic cut loose on Bolan. But lead tumblers whizzed harmlessly behind his wheels as he surged forward. Now, lined up with the driver of the assault jeep, the gap less than thirty feet, Bolan was positioned right where he wanted to be.

Bolan brought up the .44 AutoMag. He read the panic on the driver's face. Their eyes locked for an instant.

Big Thunder bellowed its death message, and a 240-grain headbuster exploded that face of terror.

The unmanned jeep bounced up over a boulder. A scream ripped across the Llano Estacado at Bolan. He saw someone make a desperate lunge at the wheel, but the vehicle flipped over the boulder, crushed down on its side. High-speed momentum sent the rig rolling like some misshapen bowling ball. Glass shattered and metal buckled.

Relentless, unwilling to give the enemy an inch of slack, Bolan bore down on the tumbling wreck. There would be survivors. And they would answer for gunning down the trooper.

Bolan's Jimmy skidded to a halt near the lip of a rise as he saw the assault vehicle vanish over the edge.

AutoMag in hand, he flung his door wide. Dust swirled into his nose. A trickle of blood ran down his forehead.

Below, a cloud of dust swirled up over the pulverized wreck. Legs splayed, he stood atop the rise like a statue, waiting.

A boot kicked the crumpled-up passenger door off its remaining hinge.

Groaning, a man slid out of the jeep's open back.

Quickly, Bolan took in the scene: three subguns and an HK-91 strewed around the battered hulk. A crate, broken open in the crash, had scattered several cone-shaped projectiles. Rocket firepower, Bolan knew. Pretty heavy weaponry for mere desert rats.

But these rats were rabid, and they came storming out of the wreckage with murder in their eyes.

One of the surviving duo lunged up over the capsized rig, his Swedish M-45 swinging toward Bolan. But a .44 slug drilled dead center through his chest, propelled him over a boulder.

Bolan sighted down the AutoMag's barrel as the man scrambled for the HK-91. Bolan let Bullet Head's fingers touch the assault rifle. Then blew him into eternity.

A ferret-faced man showed Bolan features blanched by terror. He snatched up the M-45. Rolling away from the peals of execution, the man triggered a burst that spit up dirt puffs far below Bolan. The rodent rose to his feet, tried to bolt, but the AutoMag drove him back onto the ground as if he'd been poleaxed, the slug shearing away his right biceps.

Shrieking, the guy squirmed, kicked up dust. Mind-curdling agony shook his chalk-white features.

Bolan felt nothing for the dead as he descended the hill. He thought about the families of the dead agents. And these renegades were nothing but cold-blooded murderers to him. They had caused suffering and death for many innocents.

Like the trooper on the highway.

Blood spurted from the mutilated remains of the ferret's arm. Violently, the punk's good hand shook as he pulled in the useless appendage that was his right arm.

Bolan loomed over the desert rat in the dirt.

Tears spilled down the man's face, snaked rivulets through the plastered grime on his cheeks. His teeth clenched, high-pitched cries sounded in his throat.

"Jesus—man, you killed my buddies. And I'm bleedin' to death. Help me, you b-bastard," he whined, looking as if he was ready to faint from the pain.

"Yeah, well don't consider yourself too lucky... yet," Bolan growled.

The Executioner found something loathsome about a man who would gun down another in cold blood, then grovel for mercy when his tab was due. To Bolan, the killer looked like a worm wiggling around in the dirt. Savages could expect no mercy from Bolan.

Big Thunder hung low by Bolan's side. The setting sun was a crimson orb casting long shadows down the rise, darkening the lone, tall figure.

"You got two seconds, guy," Bolan said from the shadows, his face tombstone cold, "to tell me about it. Who you are, and from where you came. Or you're not going to want to go where I'll send you next. Read me?"

The renegade glowered at Bolan with hate-filled eyes, spit. "You can suck..."

The .44 roared. The stone beside Kiley's head burst like a melon. Kiley flinched, cried out, chips pelting his face. He crabbed in desperation for a discarded M-45.

Bolan brought his boot down on the killer's lower back, pinned him.

Kiley screamed as he twisted around to look up at a face that seemed etched out of stone.

"You're gonna lose that arm. What else do you want to give up?"

Bolan let the ominous silence drag, let Kiley sweat it out some more.

"What do you want?" Kiley cried, his face ashen. "Who the hell are you?"

"Not important. Now tell me about John Engels. Is he your leader?"

Kiley froze.

Bolan could see the ferret face searching for a lie, pointed the AutoMag down at the blanched features. Bolan knew the man was slipping away from the loss of blood.

"All right...y-yeah. But...but I'm just a part of the Brigade, man...Apocalypse Brigade. I-I don't know nothing, really...man, I swear. I just patrol this desert.... We're just some dudes...."

"Engels," Bolan repeated, and his tone left no doubt about his intent. "Last chance."

"Yeah, dammit, he's who you want." Kiley forced his words out now. He turned his face away from Bolan, rested the side of his face and head on the hard-packed soil. "I don't get paid...enough for this kind of shit. I'm a vet, for chrissakes. Cut me some slack, man."

"You're dirty. And you're going to be dead if you don't tell me where Engels is. And what he's doing there."

Kiley sucked in several sharp breaths. He whimpered. "You...you gotta promise, man...you'll help me. I'm dyin'."

"Talk. I'll help."

Kiley hesitated. Pressure from Bolan's boot encouraged him.

"Th-there's...the compound...."

"Where?" Bolan growled.

"Nacimiento Mountains...hundred miles...west. Dammit, I hurt," he rasped through gritted teeth.

"Go on."

"It's twenty miles...past them stinkin' Injuns."

"A reservation?"

"No...just some shithead Injuns and an old chief that won't live on the reservation like they're supposed to."

"What's at the hardsite?"

"I don't know, I swear."

Bolan pressed down hard on Kiley's back, made the Brigade scum grunt.

"Guns . . . smack . . ."

"Heroin?"

"Yeah. Stuff brought back after Nam . . . still comin'. . . Thailand, I ain't sure . . . Engels, he uses them Injuns and greasers from across the border to load and unload . . . hates their guts . . . ain't nothin' but slave labor. A-rabs see, PLO dudes . . . they come in every coupla months for the heavy shit."

"Arms?"

Kiley swallowed hard. "Yeah."

Bolan paused for a long moment. So what Brognola suspected was true. Black market arms and heroin. Double the poison. Engels was not only financing a major terrorist organization, but supplying heroin, perhaps distributing it from coast to coast, depending on how many contacts he had, how far the pipeline stretched.

And Bolan intended to find out.

Recon and soft probe time, and if the soft probe went hard, he was ready to ram the fight down their throats, rip their guts out with his bare hands.

Bending, Bolan wrapped his hand around Kiley's shoulder, hauled him to his feet. "For someone who claimed he didn't know too much," Bolan said as Kiley cried out in pain, wobbled, "you sure made yourself out to be a liar."

The crate of projectiles caught Bolan's eye. There was a rocket launcher beside the jeep. Bolan pushed the wounded renegade away from him.

"Up the hill," he told Kiley. "Get in the Jimmy."

Bolan holstered the AutoMag. He picked up the rocket launcher. It was an RPG-7. Russian hardware. The kind of firepower the PLO liked to use in their attacks on Israeli and Western civilians. Bolan gathered the heat-seeking projectiles, tucked them under his arm.

Kiley staggered like a drunk up the rise.

For a moment, Bolan sized up his spoils of war. Yeah, some pretty damned heavy stuff. This was no ragtag band of misfits with chips on their shoulders. These cannibals were running a big operation. They had already slaughtered ten Feds and maybe one state trooper. How many more were they going to massacre, Bolan wondered.

Rage twisted the warrior's guts as he climbed the rise. Topping the hill, he opened the tailgate and slid the missiles into the wagon section of the vehicle. Then he opened the passenger door for Kiley.

The wounded man slumped against the Jimmy.

"There's a good cop back there," Bolan said, his eyes like two chips of flint behind cracked lids. "If he's dead . . . or if he doesn't make it . . ."

The warning hung in the air between them like an omen.

Kiley looked at Bolan. Fear broke through the pain in Kiley's stare. The Apocalypse Brigade member looked back down the rise at his dead comrades. He faltered on rubbery legs.

Bolan stuffed Kiley into the Jimmy.

As Bolan drove, he realized that he wanted to keep Kiley alive, have the Brigade soldier lead him to the hardsite. But Bolan was prepared to fulfill his threat if the patrolman died.

An eye for an eye.

That was the only thing a savage understood.

Still, Bolan needed the answers to some questions that troubled him. He needed to know how many hired professional guns Engels had under him. The hardsite had to be well protected or hidden or both for the renegades to have operated out on the vast New Mexico desert for so long. Perhaps the chain of traitors did reach out beyond the renegades themselves. Perhaps someone high up in the Company was involved.

Conspiracy was familiar turf to Mack Bolan. With his own hands, he had killed a KGB mole, Lee Farnsworth, in the Oval Office right under the President's nose. Farnsworth had been responsible for the attack on Stony Man Farm and the death of Bolan's greatest love, April Rose.

But that was yesterday.

And yesterday was gone. Living in the past was for men who really had nothing left to live for.

Still, Bolan knew, a man's past was as much a part of him as the present.

Kiley groaned.

Bolan looked over at the hideously wounded man. Blood soaked his brown desert khaki camos. Slouched against the door, the man had given up holding his useless arm, allowed it to hang, limp meat by his side.

Bolan found the trooper, lying motionless beside his patrol car. He hopped out of the Jimmy, strode around to the other side. There, he jerked open the door.

Kiley dropped to the dirt, grunted in surprise and pain. A delirious look in his eyes, he struggled up onto his side.

Quickly, Bolan moved to the trooper and knelt beside him.

The patrol car had been riddled by dozens of bullets. Glass from blasted-out windows was scattered over the hood and road, seat cushions had been chewed up by 5.56 mm slugs. Bolan looked at the radio, shot up by a line of fire that had drilled through the hood and dash. Steam from a ruptured radiator curled between the slits around the pocked hood. Oil dripped, soaked into the dirt.

Bolan looked at the name on the uniform. Kent Travers.

"D-dad?"

Through narrowly cracked eyelids, Travers stared up at Bolan with the strange, peaceful look of a man just moments away from death.

"Easy, Travers," Bolan consoled. "You tell me where the nearest hospital is. I'll get you there."

"F-forget it," he told Bolan in a cracking voice as he swallowed some of the blood spilling from his mouth. "I'm not gonna...make it. My...dad told me...how guys got...before...in Nam." An odd smile flickered over the trooper's mouth. "My dad... Listen...you tell him...I died like the kind...of soldier...he always wanted for a son." Suddenly, Travers reached up, clutched Bolan's arm. "He was a Green Beret...colonel...war hero...Nam. Tell him...I got it in battle.... He'd be proud." Moisture filmed the patrolman's eyes. To Bolan he seemed choked with regret.

But the warrior said nothing. He would allow this man a final few moments of deserved dignity.

Something struck Bolan then about the dying man. He couldn't have seen it before in the heat of the firefight. Now, he did. And there was something about the trooper's lean build, his brown hair and blue eyes, eyes soft even as death neared. The way Travers spoke about a father he held in hero worship...

Bolan drifted from the moment, drawn to memories of his younger brother, Johnny. Both Johnny Bolan and Kent Travers had that same fighting heart, Bolan thought. Bolan felt the hackles rise on the back of his neck. A strange chill went through him. Sorrow speared into him. He saw Johnny lying there in that pool of blood instead of Travers, wondered if...

"Gila Plains."

"What's that, trooper?" Bolan asked, his mind jolted back to the moment.

"My girl...Jamie...Gila Plains... She works there...waitress. Please...tell her.... We...we were gonna...be married."

A sigh rasped past the trooper's bloodstained teeth. His arm fell away from Bolan. His head lolled to the side.

A terrible sadness filled Bolan, weighted him to the spot. He clenched his jaw. Gently, he brushed the dead man's lids shut.

"You fought the good fight, soldier," he said in a hushed tone.

Briefly, Bolan thought about the young man's father, the fiancée he had been taken from. A man, certainly no older than Johnny Bolan, who now left behind heartache. A soldier who died in the line of duty, lost because of inexperience. A man whose hopes and dreams had just vanished with his last breath. And Mack Bolan couldn't help but wonder why good men seem to die when they are needed most by someone else.

Yeah, how many times had he seen it.

Bolan stood, turned. His piercing gaze settled on the killer of young Travers. Cold fury knotted up Bolan's guts. Grim-faced, he walked up, stood over Kiley. Slowly, Bolan drew the AutoMag from the hip holster.

Sudden fear flashed in Kiley's eyes. Pain seemed to flee from the guy like smoke swept away by a strong wind. He held up his good arm, as if this would shield him from the omen of death.

"N-no," he pleaded. "I can take you there. D-drug...l-lords. All bigshots comin' in, m-man... No!"

A flaming red sun hung behind the stone-faced man. The AutoMag bucked once in Bolan's fist. Thunder pealed away from Bolan, trailed across the desert.

Then there was only silence.

Death had come to the Land of Enchantment.

But Bolan knew that before the sun set tomorrow, he would turn this burning wasteland into a blood-bathed hell.

For Kent Travers and the woman he would have wed.

For the brave men who fought and died in the name of justice.

And for Mack Samuel Bolan, he hoped the death of many painful memories.

2

His name was Heart Sun. He was the last of the great Indian chiefs from the warrior days of Cochise and Geronimo. His face betrayed the hard passage of many summers since the Long Walk to Fort Sumner under the white eyes, Carson. Lines, as if cut by a sharp knife, crisscrossed the copper-colored flesh of his face. His eyes, penetrating and fearless, looked like two black marbles set in the hollow space above his high cheekbones. A mane of iron-gray hair framed his hawkish features, touched the sparse, sun-burnished flesh of bony shoulders.

Every day when the sun began to set, Heart Sun left his hogan in the village for his journey to the "rock of vision." Now, high atop the mesa, the ancient Navaho chief sat, cross-legged in calfskin breechcloth and moccasins, staring out at the barren plain. Twilight, with the fading sun's crimson-gold rays bathing the dark peaks and bluffs of the Sangre de Cristo range far behind him, was a time for silence, reflection.

There was power in the silence, Heart Sun knew, and power unseen in the desolation around him. If a man absorbed the silence through his ears, let it fill his spirit, then he could begin to free his heart from the trials and troubles of the world.

And silence renewed the powers of the warrior.

Through silence the warrior, the one who sought power, grew into a clearer vision of himself, the world around him. Silence made the heart still, strong.

A low wind moaned across the desert toward the Navaho chief, rattled through the brush, stirred dust. There was power in the wind, too, Heart Sun believed. The wind carried the presence of the Great Spirit, just as the Great Spirit spoke through the sunlight, the rain, the thunder and the lightning. To any who knew what to listen for.

Heart Sun knew what to listen and to look for. And he came to this mesa every twilight to seek the sign. It had become a ritual with him since the first vision of the coming of the great warrior.

Heart Sun looked at the sand painting before him. He had painted a large crow in each of the four clouds above the Rainbow Boy and Rainbow Girl. A jagged lightning bolt ripped through the center of the painting. Since the first vision, Heart Sun, like the shamans of the Great Plains Indians, had slashed his flesh a half dozen times with a knife, let the blood flow freely, soak into the dirt where the bolt of lightning was painted.

The self-inflicted torture and bloodletting was his offering to the earth, the pouring of the red water of life was the sacrifice to the Great Spirit of his and his people's suffering. He had cried out in pain and anguish many times to the Great Spirit for the deliverance of his people from the white eyes soldiers of the mountains—the *beliganos*. They had brought death, misery and treachery with their guns, their flying machines and their angry tongues.

The sand painting had never been seen by the others of his village. The holy vision that the painting represented was for his eyes only. And it also told of the persecution of his people. He had drawn chains around Navaho women and children, their bodies covered in blood, slumped in death.

Sadness touched Heart Sun. The red man was no longer free to roam the plains, hunt the buffalo. Long ago, the *beliganos* had brought their civilization to the red man.

And Heart Sun knew all about the civilization of the white eyes.

Several times he had journeyed to the cities of the white eyes. Los Angeles. San Francisco. Houston. He had traveled to these places hoping to come to an understanding about the ways of the white man; he wanted to see for himself if the Indian had surrendered his way of living to something more worthy.

Yes, Heart Sun had seen civilization. Civilization had filled the skies with choking black smoke from the automobile and the factory stacks, smoke so thick and black it threatened to blot out the sun on some days. Civilization had poisoned the streams, the lakes and the rivers with waste and chemicals, killed the fish and made the water undrinkable unless it was treated with more chemicals. Civilization had raped the land with its machines, had forced the wild animals out of their natural abode, or outright slaughtered them to make way for more civilization.

Was this civilization, Heart Sun wondered bitterly, worth what the Indian warrior once had? No, he decided, it was not. The red man had surrendered his way of life, but Heart Sun would never give up the pride and dignity of the old ways. To any man. Under any threat.

The Navaho who had left the reservation with him now tried a new way of life. They irrigated, plowed and planted. Tilling the soil was not the way of the warrior and the hunter, Heart Sun knew, but there was some freedom for a man able to live as he chose. Some freedom was better than none at all. The old ways would never return. To even pretend they would was suicide, Heart Sun knew.

His heart grew heavy. And the sorrow turned to rage when he thought about how the white eyes had not changed in their warring on the red man since the winter of Carson and the Long Walk. There was now the constant threat of the heavily armed soldiers in the Sangre de Cristo. They flew their great metallic birds of death over the desert. They rode their jeeps with their machine guns pointed at the village. They had warned Heart Sun to leave the land and return to the reservation. He had refused. This land belonged to his ancestors, and it was sacred to all Navaho. He would never be pushed around again by the *beliganos*.

But the white men did not let up in their terrorizing of the village. Two nights ago, they had stolen away some of the villagers at gunpoint. Broken Cloud and

Golden Rainbow. Little Bear and Running Elk. His children, gone, held now as hostages until Heart Sun took his people off the land that the white eyes claimed was theirs.

What was so important that the Navaho had to leave or face death? Heart Sun pondered, felt the anger knot his guts. He wanted to fight the white men, but he didn't have the support of his village. They had no weapons, except the bow, the knife and the lance. And these were no match against the weapons of the white eyes. Besides, Heart Sun knew, he was an old man, and his time was near. He had already seen his own death at the hands of the soldiers in his dreams.

Tonight, like every night since he first saw the vision in his dreams, Heart Sun waited anxiously for the crow to appear on the horizon. In his vision, the crow was as large as a condor. A terrifying caw sounded from its throat, a sound so piercing that the sun had split in half, as if in fear of the noise. Darkness then covered the land. And the warrior who was to come to deliver his people stepped out of this darkness. The warrior in his dreams came in black, but his skin was clearly white. There was great pain on the warrior's face. Pain unlike any Heart Sun had ever seen, could ever imagine a man enduring without going insane.

And in the warrior's eyes was death.

Heart Sun felt the power of the wind fill him, and he sank deeper into his spirit, calling on the vision. The ancient Navaho chief knew that all of his visions had come to pass. As a boy he had seen the Long Walk in a dream, but the elders had laughed at him. Since then, he had seen many things, many deaths in his dreams. And they had all come to pass. No one in the village laughed anymore.

Heart Sun had seen the death of the white eyes people. In his vision the warrior had vanished back into the darkness. There was blood and thunder. And then there was only ash.

Silence engulfed the ancient Indian.

The wind howled.

The great white warrior was coming soon.

Heart Sun shut his eyes. He prayed to the Great Spirit that the warrior would come before his death.

Death, Heart Sun thought, would bring him freedom, and the final peace he sought. He would be one with his blood brothers. One with the desert wind.

The wind spoke to Heart Sun. It told him that the day of reckoning for the white eyes was coming.

Death waited for no man.

Death. Heart Sun felt it now like a chill, like the touch of a finger on his shoulder.

He was unaware of the 206B JetRanger II chopper that skirted the east horizon, above the Sangre de Cristo mountain range far behind him.

DUST SWIRLED in giant brown sheets around Harold Katterhagen as he stood atop the rise, his HK-91 assault rifle in hand. The whir of the 206B JetRanger II's rotor cut the silence.

The silence of death.

And death was what stared up at Katterhagen from the deep depression in the desert floor. He was gripped by fear and surprise. And tall, lean, blond-haired, blue-eyed Harold Katterhagen, organizer of the Apocalypse Brigade, son of a major in the First SS Panzer Division, born of pure German stock in the hamlet of Lixtlenbertgern near the Elbe River, didn't like fear or surprise. He believed he was the embodiment of every trait that made up the superior German warrior. Cold. Ruthless. Calculating. Fearless. It was only a matter of time, he believed, before the world witnessed the rise of the Master Race. The Fatherland would secure its rightful place in history, achieve the greatness World War II had denied. Katterhagen would see to it. And John Engels, he knew, had the means to make his dream come true.

But now, as he watched Donald Sunther inspect the massacre, sift through the wreckage around the bodies of Stemmons and Reichler, he feared that his vision of conquest could be shattered.

Hit and run. Search and destroy. These were the guerrilla warfare tactics he had used as a Company-contracted Special Operations Division man in Central America. Know the enemy. Pinpoint his weakness, then crush him with it. That was how Katterhagen had fought in El Salvador and Honduras, even if it meant holding a bunch of frightened peasant women hostage until their menfolk walked straight into an ambush.

Katterhagen recalled how the Engels death squad had fought just that way against villages they suspected of harboring Communist-backed rebels, had used fear to bring the enemy to its knees. But fear,

Katterhagen knew, had a way of making a man stronger if he acted on it.

Someone, Katterhagen could see, was now trying to turn the fear on him. He knew that whoever had cut down his men with such brutal and lethal effectiveness was well equipped to throw Katterhagen's guerrilla tactics back in his face. Katterhagen didn't like that. Particularly when he had to answer to a man like Engels for such a loss. Engels held the key to his dreams.

The assault rifle suddenly felt heavy in Katterhagen's sweat-slippery hand as it hung low by his side. Darkness was fast settling over the Llano Estacado, and Katterhagen's gaunt face looked like a ghoul's mask in the shadows. Dirt plastered his sweat-tacky brown desert camos. The red band of the Apocalypse Brigade that he wore around his left arm was soaked with moisture, had turned dark crimson. His mind was drifting at the moment, lost in visions of world conquest and holocaust, the annihilation of Israel, and the destruction of Third World countries he believed were sucking the blood like leeches out of the strong Western world.

"What do you make of this?"

Sunther's question snapped Katterhagen out of his dark reflection. He looked down the rise at the broad-shouldered, potbellied Sunther. Sunther wasn't exactly Katterhagen's idea of the superior Aryan specimen. He felt contempt toward Sunther when he saw the expression of fear on the man's face.

"This isn't the work of any Fed," Sunther said, his voice strained in an attempt to make himself heard clearly over the whine of the chopper's rotor. "If it's Company... I thought Engels said they'd dropped that mandate. That mess was supposed to be behind us."

"The Company never forgets," Katterhagen told the man kneeling beside the headless body of Reichler. A shiver went through Katterhagen. He didn't like what was happening at all.

"They made off with that Russian rocket launcher Stemmons liked to fire off so much," Sunther groused.

"They?" Katterhagen said in an ominous tone. "How do you know it was they, Sunther? It could've been one man, for all you know."

Sunther scoffed. "One man, right."

"Colonel."

Katterhagen rested his flint-eyed stare on the man standing beside him on the rise. Ken Stanley. Stanley was a dark-haired, muscular man with a swarthy complexion, his face a deep bronze color from years of living under the harsh desert sun. Katterhagen knew that Stanley considered the desert his home and wouldn't dare think of living anywhere else. Katterhagen wondered if Stanley didn't have some Indian in his blood. It seemed strange to Katterhagen, but he accepted Stanley's love of the desert, knowing every man had his own quirks and peculiar inclinations. The desert was just a barren anus of heat and misery to Katterhagen.

But Stanley's knowledge of the Sangre de Cristo mountains had served Engels and the Apocalypse Brigade well. Stanley had led them to the ancient Pueblo ruins in the mountains that now served as their underground fortress.

Katterhagen had recruited Stanley over beers in a bar in Alamogordo, when the man told him about his Vietnam experience as a door gunner for the First Air Cavalry. They had one thing in common: a hatred for Communists and Jews. They believed these groups would be the eventual downfall of the United States, and of the world, if they weren't stopped. They believed the Communists subverted from outside the free enterprise system, while the Jews with their greed raped the system from within the guise of free enterprise.

Stanley lowered his Traq 10 x 50 binoculars. "Three klicks south. Two dead men around a Smoky's cruiser. One of them might be Kiley. I'd say we go in and double-check, but I just spotted three cruisers. Four klicks. Heading south. I'd say that means dust-off, Colonel. Time for us to fly."

Katterhagen had never served in any legitimate military. He glanced at Stanley, made a flicking noise with his tongue as if there was a bad taste in his mouth. He considered Stanley a subordinate, and resented the man calling him Colonel. Katterhagen knew and accepted what he was—a mercenary who fought for the love of money as much as he did for his love of killing Communists and Jews. Before the Company-sponsored disaster in Central America, Katterhagen had seen plenty of merc action in Southeast Asia. There, he met Engels, helped the Company man organize his opium-smuggling operation in Thailand.

Katterhagen recalled how it had been at the suggestion of Engels that the CIA had contracted him out as a paramilitary operative for the Central American operation. It had been a hasty on-the-spot decision, done out of misinformation and in desperation to do something about the Communist-backed guerrillas. Katterhagen smiled to himself. Their mistake, he thought. People get just what they deserve.

But Katterhagen knew he had to address the immediate situation, reassure Stanley and Sunther. "Look," he told them, his tone ice-cold. "We can't afford to panic and screw everything up when we're this close. There's an explanation for this, and I intend to find out what it is. Our biggest shipment is going out day after tomorrow. That means the beginning of all we've talked about. All we've dreamed about.

"Whoever killed our men, we will find him. And he will pay. I don't care if he's a Fed, or if he's Company, or..."

"We've made some enemies along the way, Colonel," Stanley cut in. "It doesn't have to be the law that's done this."

"You don't need to remind me or Engels of that."

"I think it's that old chief and some of his bucks fighting back," Sunther said, his face flushed with a rage he fought to control. "I say we go in and level that damned village like we should've done when they first started nosing around. You know the others would agree with that."

Katterhagen held up a restraining hand. A patronizing look fell over his face. "Stop and think about this for a minute, Sunther. You are foolish and impulsive at times." The German sighed.

Sunther scowled.

"First of all, I don't believe they have the type of firepower that would've done this," Katterhagen said. "You can kill a man if your worst suspicions about him are founded in fact. Yes, I want to be rid of those meddlesome—what do you call them?" he asked, stopped as if he'd just had a revelation. "Red niggers, yes. I want to be rid of those red niggers as much as you do. But we can't expect to keep our puppet strings tied to our boy much longer if we just indiscriminately start slaughtering everyone out on this hellhole. Reason, man. Think reason."

"I don't think some of the others are going to see your reason, Katterhagen," Sunther said. "They hear about this, they just might hop in one of those other choppers and go out for that Injun village on their own."

"I think it's Gordon, Colonel. I say it's time we paid our friendly Gila Plains sheriff a little visit and find out just how much he suspects. You've been putting that off too long now. Every time we've had to snuff a lawman you seem to get all bent out of shape."

Katterhagen drew a deep breath, squared his shoulders. It enraged him that his men were second-guessing him. But he knew Stanley was right. He had seen the

Gila Plains sheriff himself, scouting the canyons and arroyos near the compound with field glasses. At this point in the operation, though, Katterhagen didn't want to kill another lawman. Suspicion of their operation had already caused the deaths of three of his soldiers. Someone was on to them, he had to find out who, and fast.

"All right, then," the German allowed. "We'll go to town. 'Talk' to the sheriff. First, we fly back and get a backup unit. Just in case it is Gordon. And just in case he's alerted anyone else. Now. Let's get out of here. It's starting to stink."

Katterhagen spun away from the carnage, strode toward the JetRanger II. Dust sifted into his windpipe. All of a sudden he had a sick feeling in the pit of his stomach. He had seen Gordon in town on several occasions, judged the man to be just a back-country hick-town lawman. Certainly not a man who could deal out the sort of death Katterhagen had just seen. Besides, Katterhagen knew there was no way the sheriff's .38 could have blown the heads off the bodies he had just seen.

Somewhere out on the desert beyond him, there was a hunter, Katterhagen thought. A hunter of men.

And Harold Katterhagen wasn't accustomed to being the prey. It was a thought that made him dizzy with nausea

3

Mack Bolan found Gila Plains on the map, twenty miles southwest off Highway 44. Out of respect for a good man, he fully intended to keep his personal commitment to the slain trooper and tell the dead man's fiancée that Travers met his end bravely. Gila Plains was also in the general vicinity where the trooper's killer told Bolan the hardsite was located, give or take thirty to forty klicks in any direction.

According to Bolan's chronometer, Santa Fe was a little less than two hours behind him. Bolan knew a massive manhunt would be launched as soon as the bodies were discovered on the Staked Plain. More than 130 miles now separated Bolan from the scene of slaughter. But to avert suspicion, avoid any roadblocks, Bolan kept to the back roads, snaked a tortuous trail through the winding passes of the Rocky Mountains country in the north-central part of the state.

Now, Bolan forged ahead onto the eastern fringes of the broken, lunar landscape of the Colorado Plateau. A full moon shone down on the ominous desolation, but darkness out on the desert was always pitch-black from ground level up. Ruts and arroyos and cactus presented unseen danger to Bolan and his Jimmy, so travel was slower than he would have liked.

The uneven desert floor rose and dropped without warning, jouncing Bolan around in the cab. Headlights stabbed into the darkness, washed over the distant black lumps of mesas, the jagged knifelike shapes of sharp cliffs. This was prehistoric land, formed a million years ago by the upheaval of volcanos, shaped by the violence of molten lava plains.

Bolan hoped to find some answers in Gila Plains. Still, whether or not he had any luck there, he would recon and probe the desert. The Jimmy with its blown-out windshield and bloodstained passenger seat was now suspect, could point a finger of blame toward Bolan.

Bolan stopped in a canyon, killed the engine and doused the lights after a quick surveillance of the area. With black rock walls looming up on both sides of him like sentinels, he quickly but thoroughly cleaned the jeep free of glass. Then he took out the passenger seat, buried it in a cave.

A distant noise alerted Bolan. He froze, listening. Sound travels far in the desert, and within moments he heard the bleating noise grow into a familiar whine. Chopper.

From the Jimmy, Bolan pulled out a pair of twinned Trilux IR/4 telescopic nightsights. The infrared binocs with high-tech modification had been designed by Andrzej Konzaki, the Stony Man armorer killed in the terrorist attack on the Blue Ridge farm.

Cautious now, Bolan climbed an arroyo, feeling his way up the rock-littered path, searching the shadows and crevices. The last thing he needed was to step on a rattler, twist his ankle or stumble back down the gully and crack his head open.

He found a spot of concealment behind a line of boulders.

The chopper's rotor whined louder. Darkness and the vast sprawling terrain distorted the sound. But after a few minutes of intense listening, Bolan pinpointed the chopper to the north. There, he saw the black shape. Like some prehistoric bird it soared against the velvet, starlit sky above jagged ridges. If it was a police aircraft its search beams would have been on, Bolan knew. Instinct warned Bolan that it was no search copter.

The big guy adjusted the field vision on the binocs. Bolan saw that the big-rotored bird was an unarmed 206B JetRanger II, stripped of miniguns for civilian or commercial use. That didn't mean the passengers weren't armed, Bolan decided, an instant before he spotted the barrel of a rifle canted up against the portside window. Through the infrared device, Bolan counted three heads.

They had come east. They knew, Bolan thought. And now they were flying in the direction of Gila Plains.

The chopper disappeared into the maw of night. Silence surrounded Bolan.

There was no time to waste thinking about the action back on the highway.

As he retraced his steps to his wheels, Bolan wondered about the dead trooper's fiancée.

What was the link between the dead trooper and the renegades? If Travers had suspected something about the operation, had he told his woman anything?

If he did, Bolan knew, she was in danger.

Bolan had to get to Gila Plains. Fast. Before anyone else was pulled down by the tentacles of treachery and murder.

Bolan made it to Gila Plains when the first light of dawn broke across the sky. He parked the Jimmy deep in a fold between two hills, then climbed the hills for a quick recon.

A paved two-lane offshoot of Highway 44 cut through the center of the town's two dozen buildings, then dead-ended. Dirt roads fanned out across the brown plain toward adobe and wooden ranch-style homes. Barren, baked desolation. Mining country.

Bolan checked the town. The buildings were all single-story, made mostly of adobe to combat the fierce sun. Two old Chevy pickups were parked in front of a hitching rail at the south end of town, the frames caked with dust from rough, back-country riding. Two men sat in each of the cabs. The four appeared to be waiting. Bolan looked harder. One guy worked on a cigarette, dragging on it every few seconds as if he was nervous. Their expressions were taut, bodies rigid.

Combat senses prickled Bolan. Who the hell would be sitting in a truck waiting for anybody at this hour of the morning?

With the field glasses, he scanned the town again.

An old-timer puffed on a stogie, walked stiffly across the street in the direction of a large plate-glass window labeled Ma's Diner. The old man climbed the steps onto the boardwalk. A collie rested its head on shaggy paws, stretched out beneath an awning in front of the post office, panting, tongue lolling. A Honda scooter and several ancient-looking Ford and Buick four-doors were parked up and down the street.

A quiet scene, Bolan told himself. But he sensed something wrong, could feel it in the air. Perhaps, he thought, the town just sat on its own obvious hard luck, licking its wounds. Bolan didn't think so. What he had seen and learned so far on his desert search and destroy told him otherwise.

With his hand, Bolan brushed some of the dust out of his hair, smoothed it back. Then he wiped the dirt and splattered bugs off his face with a rag.

With Big Thunder strapped high on his hip, hidden by his sport coat, Bolan walked toward town.

"HEY. WHO THE HELL is that guy?"

"Step aside," Katterhagen told the short, thickset man with the handlebar mustache and sawed-off .12-gauge Winchester pump shotgun. The German pulled the blind back an inch. "Where did he come from?"

"Hell, I don't know. He just walked in. Cool as the breeze."

"What is it, Katterhagen?" asked a barrel-chested man with shoulder-length black hair and a bull neck from the shadows of the sheriff's office. Rising from the chair behind the large oak desk, he lifted his HK-91 assault rifle from beside the desk. "Gordon?"

"I don't know who he is," Katterhagen answered in a tight voice. "Some stranger."

The man with the assault rifle cursed. "That's great. This whole setup stinks, I tell ya. Engels warned us if we didn't grab Gordon and bring him back by midmorning he was going to take care of this himself. Sunther's probably got that chopper spinning its blades now. And if Engels sends that crazy asshole out to that village he won't just be asking polite questions."

"Shut up," Katterhagen hissed, his attention riveted on the street. He hated whiners, men who always questioned his every move. "Just keep your shirts on, dammit."

"Why couldn't Gordon have been at his home like he should've?" the brown-uniformed soldier with the Winchester pump grumbled.

"Because he knows something, that's why," Katterhagen growled.

The big man with the HK-91 sneered. "Now who's losing his cool, Colonel? Engels has got his eye on you. You screwed up by letting those Feds get too close in the first frigging place. Then you sent Stemmons and the boys down to Tucumcari to double-check on your foul-up. Big second-in-charge," he scoffed.

Katterhagen jerked his head sideways. Rage smoldered in his stare.

The long-haired man just stood behind the desk like a chunk of stone. Slowly, he nodded, several times.

"You foul up this time, Colonel, well, you know your days with Engels are numbered. 'Nuff said, huh."

"Then shut up," Katterhagen rasped. "I'm still in charge."

BOLAN WALKED DOWN the middle of the street, his strides long, smooth. The predawn darkness had turned gray during the time it took him to walk the two hundred yards to town.

Through hooded eyelids, he saw movement behind the window of the sheriff's office. Okay, he thought, so someone's watching me.

The guy in the Chevy pickup closest to Bolan flicked his cigarette into the street, followed up with a stream of spit that splattered on the road. It was a gesture of contempt, meant to show Bolan he meant nothing to them.

And these weren't just locals, either, Bolan decided. The wariness in their stares betrayed them. Glancing at the four men, Bolan read their grim, tight-lipped expressions up close. He had seen that look hundreds of times on the faces of soldiers guarding Mafia fortresses, or in the cunning stare of the predator stalking its prey, lurking in the shadows. They sure looked combat toughened, Bolan thought, and itching for action.

The pickups.

The sheriff's office.

They were waiting for someone, all right. And Bolan knew who that someone was. He'd go ahead and play whatever cards fate dealt him.

Yeah, he was walking right on top of a human time bomb.

The silence grew leaden until the squawk of a chicken broke it.

Wood groaned under Bolan's boots as he stepped up onto the planks. Rusty hinges squeaked as he opened the diner door. A cowbell tinkled, and three heads turned in the direction of the big, dirt-grimed, disheveled stranger in the doorway.

Two old-timers sat hunched over coffee at the Formica countertop. Deep-set, watery eyes. Grizzled, heavily lined faces beaten by a lifetime of hard, unrewarded labor and harsh desert sun. They looked away from the stranger after a moment of sizing him up, indifferent.

For some reason, Bolan felt his heart go out to the old-timers. Life had kicked their asses. He saw it in their eyes, their faces. They were shells in human shape, trying to forget, searching for the energy to meet the day. They'd given up on worrying about what was ahead for them. Heartache, the bitter disappointment over dreams long since broken were etched like razor slashes on the wrinkled, parchmentlike flesh of their wizened faces.

Country music droned softly from a radio beside a glass-fronted cooler. A woman crooned about loneliness and love gone cold. The song suddenly filled Bolan with a haunting sorrow. His gaze settled on the woman at the far end of the counter. He guessed she was somewhere in her late twenties. Flaxen blond hair brushed her shoulders. A white blouse with embroi-

dered red roses fit snug around her large breasts. Tan
slacks hugged her long, shapely legs. Smoke from her
cigarette curled up around the sharp, angular features
of her face.

Bolan read the warm, sincere friendliness in her blue
eyes. The look of a woman content with her life.

She didn't know yet.

Bolan's heart grew heavier with his knowledge of
the news he was about to break on the woman. He
thought about April all of a sudden, the overpower-
ing rage and grief he had felt when she'd been struck
down by the bullet meant for him.

Bolan's mouth went dry as a desert wind. His throat
felt like the rough side of sandpaper, constricting at
the terrible memory. A strange sense of disembodiment fell over him like a fog as he looked at the
woman. His mind recoiled, went back to that hellish
moment, his senses lost in a black cloud of anguish.
April's death had hacked away a part of his soul.

Her death.

Cold. Brutal. So goddamn final.

He heard the whisper of a warm voice filled with
love and longing. It called out to him from the shadowy specter of memory. His guts knotted up. The bile
in his mouth tasted like acid. The pain became all-
consuming, an unshakable force that pierced his nostrils like ammonia. An icy chill tapped his spine.
Vengeance, crushing the life out of the bastards
responsible for her death, had been a hollow victory.

Death had robbed him, ripped his heart out with its
talons. He saw her lifeless body in his lap through a

crimson haze in his mind, heard the rain crashing down around him from a sky as black as coal. The water lashed through his soul like ice needles.

"You all right, mister?"

The question hit Bolan like a fist, jarred him free of the black memories. He grunted, realizing then that he'd been staring at the blond woman.

"You look like you could use some coffee and hot food."

How was he going to tell her?

"Jamie," Bolan said calmly.

Surprise crept into her eyes. But before she could ask Bolan anything, he said, "I need to talk to you for a minute. Alone. It's about Kent."

Curious, the old-timers swiveled on their stools, looked at Bolan.

"Kent?" she said, stiffening. "Who are you? What about Kent? Is he all right?"

Bolan wanted this done in private. The moment demanded dignity.

"I knew Kent for a very brief time, ma'am. Can we talk alone?"

The woman hesitated. Her lower lip quivered. Fear shadowed her face. She suspected the worst, Bolan knew, and her instincts were dead on. This was the moment she had probably spent many lonely nights dreading, worried about her man and hating all the dangers that went with his profession.

Turning away from her, Bolan looked to the far corner of the diner. He nodded to indicate a booth toward the back wall. There was no easy way to tell her.

The woman walked past Bolan, and he followed her.

No one said a word.

The country song filled the thick silence, the singer wailing on about her broken heart.

The woman kept her attention on the big man beside her, a silent plea, a fading hope in her eyes. Gingerly, she settled down into the booth. Bolan slid in beside her. He stared through the plate-glass window at the empty street. Directly across from the diner, the shadows of dawn darkened the sheriff's office.

"What's wrong? For God's sake, tell me," she implored, her hushed voice cracking.

Bolan drew a breath. The images of April, the blood-smeared dying face of Kent Travers stayed branded in his mind.

"Jamie." Bolan looked her square in the eye. Pain knifed through him. He clenched his jaw. "Your man's dead."

4

Time stopped for Mack Bolan. His past and her present, worlds of violence and anguish, collided in what seemed like an eternity to the Executioner.

It took several long moments for the shock to finally hit Jamie. She just stared at Bolan, appeared to look right past him as if he wasn't there. She swallowed, and strangled a cry behind her tight lips. Pain turned to utter disbelief. Her hollow gaze dropped off Bolan. She clamped her eyes shut, and the tears poured over her cheeks like rainwater down a windowpane. She shivered, sobbing.

Music sounded from the radio with the sharp guitar twang of a new song. A gravelly male voice began singing about a man in a boxcar on the run from the law.

Icy rage spread through Bolan. He found himself wanting to blast that radio into a million pieces with the AutoMag.

"I'm sorry, Jamie," he said. "He was gunned down by the men I'm looking for. He didn't stand a chance against them. He thought about you and his father in his last moments."

Trembling, the woman sucked in a long breath, fighting to bring herself under control. She straightened, pressing her back against the wall, stiff as wood. Grimacing, her eyes stayed shut, as if the world was something too wretched to look at. She wiped at the flow of tears with the back of her hand, sniffling.

Bolan was silent. He knew she was trying her damnedest to stay strong, and he allowed her the dignity of her grief in silence.

Finally, she looked at Bolan. A tear broke from her eye, trickled down her cheek. A strange, wistful smile appeared on her lips. She looked away from Bolan then, as if embarrassed. "You know." Her voice cracked; she cleared her throat. "I guess I'm not really surprised for some reason. Hurt. God, I hurt.

"When Kent didn't call last night—he usually does when he gets off his shift—I got this feeling, this sick, empty feeling in my stomach. With all those dead men from the Justice Department and FBI turning up. How many nights have I stayed up, worried sick?" She sounded as if she spoke more for her own benefit than for Bolan's. She looked out across the diner, lost in troubled thought. The haunted stare faded from her gaze, and she turned her attention on Bolan. "You know, mister, we were going to be married. Did Kent tell you that?"

Bolan nodded.

She sighed. "Dreams. God, they die hard. I was so in love...so in love with that man."

April's face filled Bolan's mind. Yeah, dreams die real hard, Jamie, he thought.

And the vision of April's beautiful face exploded like a supernova through the blackness of terrible memories. Bolan fought off his rage.

"I'm carrying Kent's baby," Jamie told Bolan. "I found out yesterday. I was so excited. I couldn't wait to tell him. He's wanted a child so much. We'd made so many plans."

The men at the counter watched Jamie and Bolan. The Executioner turned them around with an icy stare. The woman's misery was not for them.

"I was going to be the perfect wife," Jamie went on. "You know, stay home. Take care of the baby. Worry about Kent. My own family was killed in a car accident when I was very young. My aunt, she raised me. But I never really had the closeness to someone I wanted." She laughed, a dry sound. "I've lived in this desert country all of my life. Never really had any desire to go anywhere else. I was so happy with Kent." Depthless sorrow filled her stare. "How can a person feel so awful empty? We had a life ahead of us. All I've got now are...memories." Her voice faltered as she said, "He was a good man."

"He was a good man, yeah," Bolan quietly said. "Jamie, there are reasons for everything. Reasons for even the worst things that happen in life. What those reasons are, none of us can ever really be sure of. Not here. Not now. But we have to stay true to ourselves, believe in our lives, hold on to hope. You hurt. I hurt for you. I once lost someone...someone I loved very much. I lost her much the same way you lost Kent. It wasn't easy, but I went on with life. She wouldn't have wanted it any other way. Kent would want the same for you.''

She studied Bolan for a moment. ''You're right,'' she said, but her voice lacked conviction. ''You're too right.''

''Listen. All that we really have in the end is what's in our hearts. The bad can make us as strong as the good, if we deal with it. In fact, the bad often makes us stronger.''

Again, she searched Bolan's face, looked deeply into his eyes. The warmth, the softness of Bolan's voice seemed to break through her grief, touch her soul.

''Who are you?'' she asked. ''Are you the law?''

''No. I'm here to find out who's killing these men. And to put a stop to it. Jamie, did Kent tell you about anything suspicious he might have seen out on the desert? Men with guns. Men in brown uniforms.''

Jamie shook her head. ''No. Except...'' She thought hard. ''Kent never really talked about his work. I knew what he did, and he knew I didn't like it....''

''Except what, Jamie? It's important I know anything that might help.''

''If you're not a Fed, then who are you?''

Bolan noted the suspicion in her voice. ''Let's just say I'm of the law, but not from it.''

She seemed to weigh Bolan's words for a stretched second before she went on. ''I overheard Kent and his father talking a couple of times. His father's commander of the state police. He was a Green Beret colonel in Vietnam. A real gung-ho hero type. Did Kent mention him?''

''Yeah. He wanted me to tell his father what happened. He seemed real proud of his father.''

''Well, proud's not exactly the word.'' Bitterness flared in her eyes. ''I'd say fear is—was more like it. I never did like that man. There's something grim, cold...distant about him. Like death haunts him.'' She shook her head, disgusted. ''He ruled Kent with an iron hand, tried to do the same with me. The man's a tyrant. Kent couldn't live up to his father's expectations. Kent wasn't the man he should've been, according to father John. He wasn't proud and tough. The bold and the brave, you know. Kent just wasn't a violent man. Far from it. He was gentle, compassionate. I don't think he could've shot anybody, even if his life depended on it. I know he joined the highway patrol for his father. The man was a hero, like a god to Kent. And all Kent wanted was for his father to be proud of him. I could see it starting to become some kind of obsession with him. It scared me at times.

''Kent's father has this real ugly streak. He seems to always know someone's weakness. He'll zero in on it. The man can kill with his tongue. I can see now why Kent's mother left his father. I don't know what Kent sees—saw in him.'' Tears glazed over the woman's eyes. She fell silent.

Bolan waited for her to go on, hoping she would tell him something crucial to his mission.

Jamie cleared her throat, sniffed back on her tears. ''Kent tried to involve himself in the investigation of those killings. He started working longer hours, double shifts. What I was going to tell you is that Kent's father told him to back off, to leave it up to the Feds. They argued about the Indians, too."

"Indians?"

"Yeah. The Navaho. They live about thirty miles from here out on the desert. They don't want to live on the reservation. For some reason that always seemed to make Kent's father uptight. I don't know why. God," she cried. "I wish I knew why to any of this. Why? Why?" she implored, as she grabbed her hair, hung her head.

Bolan shared the woman's pain. He wished he had answers to her questions. And he intended to find out.

"I'm going to have this baby," she said with sudden conviction. "I'll do the right thing. I'll raise the baby myself if I have to. You were right, mister, whoever you are. I have to go on. Kent would've wanted it that way. That's the kind of man he was."

Bolan showed the woman a warm smile. "I'm sure you'll do the right thing, Jamie. It takes guts. For whatever it's worth, I can see you have that."

Yeah, go on with it, woman, Bolan thought. Whoever's responsible for all this, they'll pay. The warrior made an oath to himself to search every inch of that desert, turn up every damned rock if necessary to crush these snakes.

The cold worm of vengeance consumed Bolan. Life was just too damned precious to him to let good people suffer at the hands of bad men. Someone had to stand up, had to be willing to make sacrifices in order to right injustice, even if that meant risking one's own life to the ultimate. What good was a world if men didn't act to make it better?

Forget the hero rhetoric.

Forget the pillars of example and righteousness crap.

Forget the personal glory and the glory of man. It all turned to ashes and dust in the end anyway. But the end wasn't here yet, and the moment had to be dealt with.

Confront the cannibals.

Just then movement out on the street caught Bolan's attention, pulled him out of his thoughts.

A jeep drew up in front of a building next to the sheriff's office. Bolan watched as the door opened. A tall man with a brown Stetson and gun belt, a man as lean as a whip, stepped out of the vehicle.

"That the sheriff?"

"Y-yeah," Jamie stammered, still caught in the throes of her anguish. "Jim Gordon. What—are you going to tell him?"

Combat senses alerted Bolan. His face went as hard as mountain rock.

"What's wrong?" Jamie asked, alarmed by Bolan's look.

The sheriff put his hand on the knob of his office door.

Instinctively, Bolan's hand inched toward the bulge on his hip beneath the sport coat. "Stay here."

The woman hesitated, then slid out of the booth and followed Bolan.

FORTY-YEAR-OLD SHERIFF JIM GORDON wasn't accustomed to trouble. Once a year the outlaw motorcycle gang, the Lone Wolves, would cut a swath through Gila Plains on their run from San Bernardino to New Orleans for Mardi Gras. They would get rip-roaring drunk, pick fights with the local toughs and maybe even fire off a few Magnum rounds on the outskirts of town. But Gordon always handled the scene like any small-town sheriff out in the middle of nowhere would.

Lie low, turn the other cheek and, if worse came to worst, just down a few brews with the punks to let them know he wasn't such a bad dude, even if he was The Man. The local whore, Patsi, always helped to keep the whole scene under control, too.

Yeah, biker trouble Sheriff Jim Gordon could handle. What he couldn't handle was a paramilitary-style unit of brown-uniformed soldiers flying gunships over his desert and riding the wasteland in jeeps with tripod-mounted .50-caliber machine guns.

Gordon had taken a long ride in his jeep out into the desert, just to shut up a raving old hermit who still believed there was gold out in the hills. And the sheriff had seen it all. Two days ago. Crates pulled off a cargo plane on an isolated runway near the mountains where the ancient Pueblo ruins were. Navaho, and Mexicans who he knew were illegal aliens, carried the crates through the prehistoric catacombs of the Nacimiento Range like slaves under the threatening stares of heavily armed white men. "Beliganos," the Navaho called them.

Sniper fire had tracked Gordon halfway through the valley.

And he was scared, to the point where he'd made up his mind to do something about it all. And that was to alert the FBI in Sante Fe and let them handle it. They were big-time. He wasn't. They could take care of it if anyone could.

Then Gordon began thinking about the dead agents who had been found in the north and southeast parts of the state. There was some connection there, he feared.

Sweat beaded on Gordon's furrowed brow. His heart thumped like a wardrum in his ears. His chest hurt, and a fierce tension headache felt as if it would pump his brains right out of his ears.

Gordon didn't notice the men in the Chevy pickups. As he opened the door to his office he wasn't aware of anything but his own growing panic.

What if they'd seen him? What if they were after him? They weren't just some good old boys playing weekend mercenary.

A hand shot out of the blackness, grabbed Gordon by the arm.

Two faces flashed in the sheriff's sight as he twisted away from his attacker. Gordon reacted out of fear and terror, out of all the visions of death and doom that had filled his mind for the past forty-eight hours. His hand streaked for his .38 Smith & Wesson with a lightning quickness that surprised even him.

It sure surprised the three shadows in his office. They reacted instantly. Sheriff Jim Gordon didn't.

"Don't do it, Gordon!" Katterhagen shouted.

"Stupid pig!" the man beside the German rasped. And cut loose with his HK-91.

A Winchester pump shotgun also erupted, parting the shadows with smoke and flame.

"No!" Katterhagen roared.

Too late.

A deadly hailstorm of .12 gauge buckshot and a burst of .308 tumblers lifted Gordon off his feet, hurled him back through the window like a scarecrow in a hurricane.

5

A violent noise shattered the peaceful dawn of Gila Plains.

Glass exploded, and the lifeless buckshot- and bullet-shredded remains of Sheriff Jim Gordon thudded onto the wooden planks of the boardwalk.

Bolan threw back the diner door. Big Thunder filled his hand. He saw three men bolt through the blown-out window opening, one after another, weapons poised, tracking.

Jamie and the two old-timers froze behind Bolan, three pairs of eyes wide with fear and shock.

The Chevy engines gunned to life. Tire rubber smoked, screeched. The two pickups shot out into the street, nearly colliding in reverse.

Bolan took in the scene in a heartbeat, combat ready.

Battle-trained reflex launched Bolan into the firefight.

Big Thunder spit a 240-grain round, the slug drilling dead center through the chest of the guy with the Winchester pump. The smoking, flaming shotgun unleashed a charge that tunneled up through the awning above him. Wood splintered skyward as Bolan's opening round propelled the shotgunner back into the darkness from where he came.

Two HK-91s chattered. Return fire swept toward Bolan.

Bolan sensed rather than saw Jamie standing behind him, right in the line of fire. The soldier reacted instantly, became a wink of blinding movement. Spinning, he grabbed the woman, shielding her with his body.

A Buick four-door sat less than three feet to Bolan's left, but it seemed like an unreachable distance in the heat of the firefight. Fury over the slaughter of the sheriff and fear for the woman's life filled Bolan as he flung Jamie sideways.

Bolan and the woman tumbled, a tangle of arms and legs, to the street behind the Buick.

The old-timers dived to the floor, covering their heads.

The two Brigade members stood, splay-legged on the planks, assault rifles hammering out a killing fusillade.

Twin lines of .308 hornets blazed over Bolan and the woman. Slugs whizzed past the Executioner, raked his cover relentlessly.

The leaden hurricane obliterated the diner door and plate-glass window. The Buick's windows, punched out by the onslaught, showered glass down on Bolan. Flying fragments sliced across the skin on the Executioner's face like tiny razors. Shards of glass blew over the old-timers in deadly waves.

Return fire kept Bolan pinned down. At the moment his main concern was keeping Jamie alive. And their survival hinged on his immediate response to the assault rifles.

Bolan saw the lead pickup angle toward him. An assault rifle poked out of the passenger window, the face behind the HK-91 twisted with murderous intent.

The Executioner's stainless-steel hand cannon poked up over the Buick's right front fender. Bolan triggered a round that splattered the gunner's head all over the cab. The assault rifle dropped from lifeless hands, clattered to the street.

Hellfire kept pouring over Bolan. The battle had just started to heat up.

The Executioner fired again. A .44 slug exploded through the windshield of the front-running truck, ripped out the driver's throat. Blood jetted from the gaping maw in the man's neck, bathed the cab until it looked like some abstract painting.

Bolan braced himself for what came next. He covered the woman as the unmanned pickup rammed into the Buick's back end, whipping the car sideways. Metal tore and glass chunks sprayed over Bolan like a mine blast.

Then, the ice-eyed hellfighter used the precious split second the tremendous collison allowed to trigger another round toward the assault tandem across the killzone.

And the Executioner found blood and took life from the man with the long scraggly black hair. The leftover hippie vanished into the sheriff's office as if a wrecking ball had slammed into his chest.

Another HK-91 opened up to Bolan's left. But the line of fire was cut short as the lead Chevy careened into the path of the second pickup.

In wild desperation, the driver stomped on the gas pedal, threw the wheel hard, away from Bolan.

Desperate, but not good enough.

The pickups hammered into each other.

Two thunderous explosions erupted from Bolan's AutoMag. The first slug tunneled through the gunner's ear, the upward path of the high-velocity skull-buster shearing off the top half of his head. He joined the driver, wedded in bloody death, when the second screaming bullet found its mark.

As if it had a mind of its own, the pickup raced toward Katterhagen. The German flung himself to the boardwalk. The pickup plowed through the railing like a rampaging rhino. Planks crushed, shot up beside the truck's frame as the Chevy and its gruesome cargo rammed through the wooden front of the sheriff's office. The awning toppled as the runaway block of metal tore into the building.

Bolan checked Jamie. Frightened eyes sought out the Executioner. She stared up at Bolan, dazed, but otherwise unharmed, he noted. Behind him, the old-timers crabbed for the far corner of the diner, seeking deeper cover.

Bolan sat the woman up against the tire, shielding her from any bullet that could ricochet off the street from underneath the carriage.

Katterhagen slammed a fresh clip into his HK-91, slithered free of the rubble that buried him.

Bolan heard the scrape of wood, the crunching of glass. He tasted the bitter, salty flow of blood in his mouth. The streak of crimson ran from a gash in his forehead where glass shrapnel had found its mark.

Bolan eyeballed the faces chancing a look out into the hellzone from windows and doorways on both sides of the street.

"Get inside!" Bolan ordered the townspeople, saw faces duck out of sight. "Stay down," he told Jamie, then, crouched, slid down the side of the battered Buick.

Katterhagen triggered a long burst, raking the car from front to back, aiming beneath the car's frame.

Bolan threw himself up against the back tire as slugs punched into metal, whined off the asphalt. Air hissed from punctured tires, stray slugs cutting across the tar, bouncing up into the undercarriage.

Jamie grimaced against the rain of glass chips that pelted her.

"Don't move," Bolan rasped.

Silence.

Bolan heard the crunch of debris. The killer was going for deeper cover or making his way to the truck, Bolan knew. And Bolan had no intention of letting the situation turn into a standoff, or letting the blond killer get away.

A moment later the enemy made the decision for Bolan.

The Chevy's engine revved.

Bolan raised the AutoMag, prepared to deliver a final headshot. Then a flashing light snared his attention. Turning his head he saw a patrol cruiser speeding toward town, two hundred feet down the road and bearing down hard.

The Chevy burst out of the wreckage in reverse.

Bolan leaped to his feet, sighting down the Auto-Mag.

But there was no sign of the Apocalypse Brigade killer.

Hunched low on the seat, Katterhagen sent the truck barreling on a frenzied squeal of tire rubber toward Bolan's cover.

Pain and panic cut Jamie's face when the big man with the hand cannon snatched her, hauled her away from the potential death trap.

Bolan threw the woman across the boardwalk with all his strength. As he dropped down on top of her, the Chevy's back bumper impacted squarely into the Buick's side doors. Metal caved in like tinfoil against the triphammer force of the collision, and the Buick flipped over. Shock waves jolted Bolan as the wreck crushed down on its roof. The boardwalk splintered and wood shot out in all directions, three feet from where Bolan smothered the woman.

The lawman now became Bolan's prime concern. Men of the law, both local and federal, were considered soldiers of the same side. To bring one down by his own hand would compromise Bolan's fight for justice. And Bolan didn't plan on changing that now, or ever.

Still, he wondered how the patrolman had gotten to the scene so quickly, or was it just coincidence? Were backup units on the way?

Bolan knew he had to get the hell out of town. Fast.

"You all right?" he asked Jamie, glass needles jabbing into his arms and legs.

Lamely she nodded, then looked in the direction of the oncoming cruiser. "You'd better get out of here," she said as the cruiser skidded, swung sideways.

Bolan stood, drew a bead on the fleeing Chevy. The driver stayed hidden, low on the seat, zigzagging the truck back and forth across the street in a reckless attempt to avoid Bolan's fire.

Turning his attention back to the lawman, Bolan saw the trooper fling the cruiser door wide. The distance was less than thirty feet, and Bolan knew the pump shotgun the lawman pulled out of the cruiser could turn him into a bloody sieve.

"Hold it!" the lawman yelled, leveling the pump shotgun through the space in the open door, the car protecting him from any sudden rounds.

But Bolan didn't fire. And he didn't give that man a chance to use his weapon. With catlike grace and speed, Bolan plunged through the jagged shards of the diner window, covering his head and face with his arms.

"No!" Bolan heard Jamie cry from behind him as he bolted through the diner.

Shaking from fear, Jamie stood, braced herself against the doorjamb. "He saved my life, John," she pleaded in a high-pitched voice.

The powerfully built lawman, his square face contorted in a rage, his dark eyes blazing fiercely, charged toward the diner. "Out of my way, girl!" he bellowed, face flushed crimson.

Jamie stood in the doorway. Grim determination hardened her features. "Don't kill him. You don't know what happened."

"I said get out of my way, Jamie," the trooper snarled, then swept her aside.

Jamie stumbled, tripped over a jutting strip of cracked floorboard and fell.

Shotgun low by his hip, the lawman gave the devastation inside the diner a quick look. "Jesus," he breathed, then moved toward the flapping kitchen doors.

Bolan sprinted up the barren rise toward the hills overlooking Gila Plains, the AutoMag back in hip leather now. Loose gravel crunched beneath his pounding boots. Sweat plastered the hair to his forehead, washed away the telltale bloody signs of battle.

Bolan turned, saw the lawman pop out of the back doorway of the diner. The shouted curse that reached Bolan's ears betrayed to him the lawman's frustration at being unable to bring him down with the shotgun; Bolan quickly lengthened the distance between them.

When Bolan reached his Jimmy, he found everything as he had left it. Then he searched the plain, spotted the cloud of dust that trailed the Chevy. The truck sped north, vanished behind a low range of hills that bubbled out of the desert floor.

Bolan turned a steely-eyed gaze back to the carnage.

The big lawman showed himself on the street. He raved at Jamie.

Straining his ears, Bolan heard, ''I'll deal with you later, girl.''

The familiarity with which the lawman addressed Jamie in his fit of rage led Bolan to believe he'd just encountered the father of the slain trooper.

Intently, Bolan watched as the officer hopped into his cruiser, gunned the engine.

John Travers now posed a serious, if not crippling, threat to Bolan's mission. And the Executioner had to stop any immediate pursuit if he was going to lose himself in the desert for a thorough recon.

Slowly, Bolan slid the AutoMag from its holster. As the cruiser gained speed, he dropped into a marksman's crouch. Sweat burned into Bolan's eyes, made him blink several times. He steadied his gun hand, his ice-blue eyes glittering like diamonds behind slit lids.

The cruiser tore beyond the north end of buildings.

Bolan sighted, squeezed the trigger.

Three times.

Three echoes of rolling thunder.

And three tires blew.

The cruiser skidded out of control. Bolan guessed the trooper thought he was under attack. The Executioner fed the lawman's panic, sent two more rounds from the AutoMag.

A spiderweb cracked across the front windshield, the .44 slug drilling harmlessly into the passenger seat a microsecond before the other high-velocity slug shattered the rear window.

Wildly the cruiser spun, jounced down into a ditch.

Bolan's final round exploded through the grill. A rising plume of steam told the Executioner he'd found the radiator. Satisfied that the vehicle was completely disabled, Bolan stood. Grim-faced, he waited, the AutoMag hanging by his side.

Several seconds dragged.

Finally, Bolan saw the door open.

The lawman got out of the car, dropped behind the door for cover. A revolver showed in his hand.

"Give it up, mister!" the lawman shouted. "You'll never make it out of this desert. I could have twenty units here in thirty minutes. You hear me?"

Bolan listened as the angry words echoed through the hills behind him.

"This is Colonel John Travers, mister. Commander of the New Mexico State Police. You listen to me good, you murdering bastard. My son's dead. And I got this feeling that I'm looking at the son of a bitch who did it."

"All you have to do, Travers," Bolan called down to the man, "is check out the ballistics on those slugs that cut your boy down. There were three other men at that scene."

Silence.

Bolan knew his words had registered.

"You just let the killer of that sheriff get away, Travers. I intend to hunt him down. And anyone else who's involved. Right now, I'm getting some very bad gut feeling myself. You'll do us both a favor by staying out of my way."

"What the hell's that supposed to mean?"

Travers waited for an answer, but Bolan didn't respond.

The big hellstormer holstered the .44 AutoMag, turned and walked toward his Jimmy.

Travers flew into another rage. "I don't know who the hell you are, mister, and I don't know why that girl got in my way and kept me from blasting you into eternity. But I'll tell you this."

Bolan opened the Jimmy's door, slid into the cab. He fired up the engine.

"I'll be the one who's doing the hunting. You hear me?"

Bolan heard; he didn't listen.

The 4x4 eased out from between the fold in the hills.

Travers stepped out into the middle of the road.

Dust trailed Bolan down the rise. He drove away from Travers, cut across the two-lane road and headed out into the desert. Looking into his sideview mirror, he saw Travers shaking his fist.

"I swear, you . . ."

The vast desert sucked up the trooper's threat.

A rumbling stirred deep in Bolan's guts. A deep sense of foreboding darkened his thoughts. He wasn't even twenty-four hours into his mission, and already a massive police manhunt was about to descend right on top of the Colorado Plateau.

Right on top of Mack Bolan.

The desert sky lightened as the new day neared.

But the Executioner knew his future was turning blacker by the minute.

6

Crowbars pried the lids off the wooden crates piled in the six trucks. The sun had not yet cleared the mountain range to the east, and deep shadows bathed the tall figure of John Engels. The renegade operative watched the Navaho and Mexicans unload the crates under the fixed muzzles of HK-91s and Colt M-16A1 Commandos.

Engels inspected the cache of newly acquired arms. A cunning gleam brightened the outlaw's dark stare. His personal cadre of soldiers, sent out in choppers and light twin-engine aircraft, always acquired these weapons through deals Engels set up with black-market arms dealers deep in Mexico and Central America.

A little cash and a lot of uncut scag, he knew, went a long way in whetting the greed of warlords and drug kings anxious to turn easier and bigger money.

Engels tempted them with the pure heroin his men smuggled out of Thailand and Cambodia in collusion with the Khmer Rouge regime. An uncut kilo from the poppy fields of Southeast Asia would net more than five hundred thousand dollars on the streets of America.

Heroin was definitely a more lucrative venture than arms dealing, Engels had decided long ago. This was what he'd always convinced his gunrunning contacts over the past several years.

But when these deals went down and the time for the trade-off came, Engels's soldiers turned the weapons they'd purchased on the gunrunners—men Engels had done business with during his years as a military adviser in Vietnam and later during his brief stint as a contracted paramilitary operative for the Company.

And for war-hardened guerrilla fighters, the slaughter of these unsuspecting gunrunners was always easy. Engels kept the opium he had promised to deliver. But more important, he seized the weapons without losing a dime or a kilo brick. Engels would then jack up the price on the arms and double his profit by selling to terrorist groups he knew were in a desperate search for firepower.

Death. Destruction. Money. They meant total power to John Engels. Seizing. Killing. They left more room in the world for Engels to move about freely, without having to fear for his life. And nothing of any real value would ever fall into undeserving hands.

Engels believed he was a noble warrior, conquering and ridding the planet of inferiors, who would topple the Western world with their weakness, their inability to sustain themselves. Only the strong, he often told his men when pumping them up with his hate propaganda, should inherit the earth. There were fortunes to be made by strong men. There were inferiors to be slaughtered by those with the vision. There were great conquests ahead for all of them.

Engels looked at the grim, sun-burnished faces of his soldiers. All of them, except Stanley, had been with him near the end of the farce Engels called Vietnam. That war, like the United States now, had been run by spineless, self-serving men, he believed, and the entire disaster in Southeast Asia had been one long adrenaline rush for the Company. But Engels recalled the body counts, the power he'd been given by the Company to move about like a shadow of death and create clandestine behind-the-lines missions for Special Forces. The whole experience had excited him as nothing else ever had.

Engels reasoned then, that if the gutless politicians and the self-glorifying military hierarchy could benefit from prolonging the slaughter of young American troops and Vietnamese, then he had a right to take a piece of that action, too. Indeed, if death could make some milk-livered pencil pusher's purse fatter, then a man who had his nose right there in the blood and guts had twice that right.

The disgruntled, disillusioned soldiers he'd sought out had felt the same way. War was indeed hell, but a man could cut himself a slice of heaven out of it if he made the right moves at the right time—like selling stolen U.S. arms to Charlie in exchange for opium, as Engels had done.

"You are dead-on about the Cuban dealer, Captain," Stanley said in congratulation, lifting an RPG-7 launcher from one of the crates.

Sunther picked up an AK-47, held and examined it like a child at Christmas with a new toy. He whistled. "How much you think you'll get from those sand niggers for these sweet babies?"

"My man in Jordan said two grand per automatic. Not bad. But not quite what I wanted. Of course, it's the grenade launchers they're most interested in. I plan to do some finagling to get what I want."

"You always do, Captain," Stanley said, smiling. "The light of reason, right? They'll see that when they get here."

"Yeah, when those ragheads see that stockpile we got waiting for them, they'll see the light of reason, all right."

"You know, Captain," Stanley said, his brow furrowed, "so far you've pulled all the right strings. I gotta say, I'm impressed at how easy it's been for us. I just hope our luck don't sour. We keep pulling those hit and runs like we did in Costa Rica and you can bet we'll end up on the shitlist of every terrorist group, intelligence and law enforcement agency the world over. There won't be a rock big enough or a jungle thick enough to hide us."

"That doesn't concern me, Stanley, and it shouldn't concern you either," Engels said, voice hard, eyes cold. "First of all, I've been doing this for thirteen years. The key to my success has been the ability to cover my tracks. Something the Company taught me and these others all too well. Second, I hate having to deal with those sand niggers, too. But their money's good. And they pay on time.

"They're the only ones we have to deal straight with. The Communist scum, those peasants in El Salvador and Honduras you've terminated, are better off dead. They were just parasitic beings, taking up much-needed space in this world. Taking all and giving nothing. However, we need our PLO contacts."

Engels's jaw jutted, his eyes burning with sudden ferocity.

"They're damned close now to bringing those Jews to their knees."

"Begging your pardon, Captain," Stanley said, "but they ain't really no closer now to all that than they were in '67, when the Israelis rolled right over the Syrians at the Golan."

Engels jabbed a finger in Stanley's direction, like a father scolding a disobedient son.

"That's where you're wrong," he continued. "What do you think I've been training you men for? Why do you think I've been dumping these shipments onto the Arabs? Why do you think they come to me before they do the Russians? Why, huh? Answer me that?"

Stanley stood in silence.

The brown-uniformed soldiers seemed paralyzed.

"I'll tell you why. Because they know I believe in their cause. Totally! And I intend to be there, Stanley—all of us will be there when Israel is finally wiped off the face of this earth. I don't expect you to understand the importance of any of this. You're getting paid. And paid well. Sometimes, I think, too well. Just do your job."

"Yes, sir, Cap'n."

Engels kept his stern gaze trained on Stanley for several moments. He didn't like the guy's insubordinate nature, his flippant attitude. But Engels knew he couldn't expect any man who was not of pure German blood to understand the urgent need for the master race to triumph and set the world in order.

Before it was too late.

Hitler was right, Engels believed with a vengeance, when he told his people that the Jews—which he, Engels, considered a shrewd, greedy, miserly people—had been responsible for the economic ills Germany suffered following World War I. History didn't lie. Facts spoke for themselves; it was the instinct for self-preservation. Each race of men was blessed, or cursed, with certain traits that distinguished it from all the rest.

The Company, Engels remembered, had called him a "blind man," dismissed him because of his racist views. Engels wouldn't even consider the fact that it was his campaign of genocide in Central America that had led to his downfall.

A liquidation mandate had been issued by the Company on Engels and his death squad. Later that mandate was lifted for reasons Engels could only guess. He supposed that some yellow journalist had dug up incriminating evidence about the massacres in the peasant villages in the lower Americas.

The termination of Engels and his men would have only been proof positive that the Company was linked to the slaughter. And the Company, Engels knew from long, hard experience, had plenty of ways to cover its own tracks. The best way was to deny knowledge that any errant operative ever worked for them. And since special ops were never directly employed by the CIA, rather contracted outside of the agency or loaned directly by the armed services, it was an easy task for the Company to lie about wrongdoing on the part of its operatives.

What really galled Engels was the gullibility of the American press, the naíveté of the American people. The average citizen just didn't want to believe that his hands were getting dirtied and bloodied in secret wars that his tax dollars ultimately paid for. The bleeding heart, lily-livered politicians had voters to answer to. And those voters didn't want to hear that their government had to wage war as ruthless and dirty as the bad guys.

Joe American wanted to keep his manicured suburban lawn and two-car garage from being leveled by the hammer and the anvil, but he didn't want to do a goddamn thing about it. Except moan about all the injustice in the world. Pontificating bastards.

It was a contradiction. It was a double standard. Worst of all, it was a lie. Let me keep what I have, Engels heard his mind say in mockery of all Americans, but don't let me know what you're doing to let me keep what I have. I just want to stay in my ivory tower where everything is warm and sweet.

Just thinking about the complex issues of the world threw Engels into a murderous fury. All the double-talk and empty, patronizing political speeches he'd heard . . .

What it boiled down to in the end, Engels thought, was every man for himself. Dog eat dog. And beat those dogs into simpering, bloody submission was just what John Engels intended to do. He would start with Israel, then move on to the parasitic Third World countries, he decided.

He'd seen enough.

He'd heard enough.

It was time to act.

Time to conquer and seize.

Time to burn and annihilate.

Anarchy.

Total and absolute.

That was the only way to reestablish order in a world gone mad.

"Hey, Cap'n. Look," Stanley suddenly said.

As a group, Engels, the brown-uniformed soldiers and the Mexicans and Navaho turned their attention toward the mouth of the gorge.

"Katterhagen." Sunther said the man's name like a curse. "Where are the others?"

"My thoughts exactly," Engels muttered, his eyes taking on a strange, distant look.

The Chevy pickup came to an abrupt, dust-spewing halt in front of Engels.

Instantly, Engels noted the fear masking the features on Katterhagen's face. Something was wrong, Engels knew. Very wrong.

"Now what the hell's happened?" Engels barked as Katterhagen stepped out of the truck.

"We've got trouble," Katterhagen said, the breath rasping out of his flared nostrils as he stood, stiff with obvious terror, before Engels. "Some bastard just blew through that town. He had this goddamn cannon, I tell you. Just blew the others away like they were fuckin' nothin'."

Engels's eyelids narrowed. A dangerous gleam lurked in his stare. "What?"

"We went in to grab Gordon, like I told you, right?" Katterhagen went on in a rush. "This morning this son of a bitch just appears out of nowhere like...like some fucking devil. Cool as ice. Gordon finally shows. He panics and goes for his piece. Turner and Marshal blow him away. Next thing I know that bastard's out of the diner and dropping our guys with that cannon like they were just green punks."

"What bastard?" Engels growled. "Slow down, damn you. Describe him."

"Jesus," Katterhagen said, flustered, running a trembling hand through his hair. "Hell, he was tall. Dark hair. He had these eyes like ice, that's what I remembered most when I first saw him walk into town. That piece of his wasn't any cop or Fed's gun, that much I know. After checking Stemmons and the others last night, there's no doubt in my mind it's the same guy."

Engels turned away from Katterhagen. He searched his mind, racked his memory. Something began to click. Something terribly, deadly wrong. Ice eyes. Tall. Loner. Big gun. Vietnam! The Executioner!

"Bolan," Engels breathed.

"Who?" Katterhagen asked, tentative.

"Mack Bolan," Engels snarled at Katterhagen. "That's who you just described. The Executioner, they called him in Nam. Among other things. Like Sergeant fuckin' Mercy."

"How..." Katterhagen mumbled.

"I saw the guy once over there. He was one of those hotshot behind-the-lines sniper marksmen. Had an outfit he called Sniper Team Able. They were supposedly the best. And the enemy body count they racked up proved it. Damn!"

"Bolan?" Katterhagen said, his face clouded by dark thoughts. "The same Bolan that took on the Mafia by himself?"

"And damn near wiped every one of them out."

"It couldn't be," Sunther said. "Bolan, I heard, is dead."

"Well, you heard wrong," Engels growled. "It's Bolan."

Engels chewed on memories. He had heard plenty about Mack Bolan. Most of it was after Vietnam. The soldier's father had gone berserk when he'd discovered his daughter selling her body to pay back some Mafia loan sharks. Old man Bolan killed his family, shot himself.

Mack Bolan had then gone on a one-man crusade to exterminate the Mob. And damn near succeeded in putting them out of business for good. Bolan's government-sanctioned operations against world terrorism as Colonel John Phoenix was no secret. Engels had gotten wind of Bolan and his Phoenix Force and Able Team through the far-reaching grapevine of Company intelligence. Engels knew there'd been a Company liquidation mandate against Bolan, an order to "terminate with extreme prejudice" because of his renegade actions. That mandate had been lifted for reasons Engels wasn't certain about.

Now the bastard was knocking right on his back door, guns blazing. There could be no other answer, Engels thought, feeling a surge of panic in his belly. There was just no one else capable of wreaking the cold-blooded havoc he'd heard about during the past twelve hours.

And they were so close. So damn close now.

"What are you going to do, John, if it is this Bolan?"

Engels looked at Mike Spencer, then searched the faces of his men now gathered around him. He read the fear in their eyes. They seemed like cornered animals to him. He wanted to scream in their faces, "Where the hell are your guts?"

But Engels knew he had to get control of the group. Somehow. Fast.

"If Salviche and Bozzarelli get word of this they may split. That means the whole deal goes right down the toilet."

Engels thought about the East Coast druglords Kyle Mervin mentioned. The druglords were there now, waiting with their muscle deep in the catacomb where the scag and arms were stockpiled.

"They're chickenshit, those two," Mervin went on. "They hear about this..."

"Well, they're not going to hear about it," Engels snapped. Then he turned back to Katterhagen, stuck a finger near the blond man's face. "You screwed up again, didn't you? You kept letting Stemmons and them joyride all over the state. You kept telling me it was easier to dump those bodies far away. Now, I've got the biggest deal yet going down, something I've worked and planned for night and day for two years, and this whole operation just might blow up in my face."

Katterhagen held his arms out, palms up. "Hey, he's just one man, John."

"One man, my ass!" Engels roared. "Shows me how much you know about what's going on sometimes."

The silence in the gorge became leaden.

The renegade PM leader's menacing stare burned into Katterhagen.

A low chuckle broke the threatening hush.

Engels whirled, eyes flashing with the hatred he felt torching his soul. It was one of the Indians, Running Elk, Engels believed his name was, who had dared to laugh.

The white men stepped aside, let Engels pass between them.

"You find something amusing about all of this, Indian?"

Engels towered over the broken, beaten slaves he used for duties around the compound. They looked so wretched, so inhuman to him. Pitiful creatures, he thought, just staring. Like living dead men. Zombies.

Their eyes, bloodshot and watery, were sunken like black pools in hollow-ringed holes. Dirt seemed permanently ingrained into the sparse, sun-ravaged flesh of faces that looked like cracked leather hide. Their naked shoulders sagged, their bare backs humped from hauling the heavy crates for the past several months. Hideous-looking scars from severe whip lashings streaked their backs.

They were all "inferiors" to Engels. He enjoyed their suffering—it made him feel strong, powerful. And they would all die following the trade-off. Engels couldn't suppress a grin as he thought about the months they had toiled under the brutal sun, erecting the barracks, clearing the airstrip. All of it for nothing now, because Engels and his men would leave that hellhole soon. In his mind Engels worked out the death of each Indian. The snake pit. Death by burning. Even now, he anticipated their shrieks, envisioned their bodies writhing in agony at his hand.

But Engels felt his wrath build toward explosion, like the fuse on a dynamite stick burning low. For he found no fear in their eyes. Instead, he saw defiance. And contempt. He realized then that he'd broken everything but their spirit. And the spirit was the first thing, he knew, that had to be broken in a man before total control was given over to the captor, the "superior."

"The warrior has come for your destruction, *beligano*." Running Elk spoke clearly, his tone low but firm. A look of triumph lit his eyes. He drew himself erect, squaring his shoulders. "Your vision of conquest will be broken. My people will be freed. You dreamed the dream of a fool."

It was too much for Engels to bear. He lashed out with a backhand that cracked like a pistol shot across the Indian's mouth. It was a terrible, lightning blow, thrown with all the force Engels could put behind it. It should have dropped Running Elk on his back.

But the Indian still stood, tall, proud. Hatred blazed in his dark eyes. He let the blood trickle down the side of his mouth. "You are a brave man, *beligano*, with your guns and soldiers. But your time is near. Heart Sun has spoken. Many times."

"Yes. That old chief. Your people," Engels spit with disdain. "You know what I think, Indian? I think maybe some of your fine bucks told that sheriff something. I think it's time my men paid your village another visit. Only this time I'll make my intentions clear. Very, very clear. And before I leave, Indian, before I leave this hellhole, I'm going to drop your scalp, personally, right in that old chief's lap."

A demonic smile slid over the lips of the Apocalypse Brigade's leader.

"Sunther. Stanley," Engels called over his shoulder, but kept his stare fixed on Running Elk. "Get those choppers ready. Take Wilson, Rankin and Peters. I want you to fly to that stinking village. This time make my warning heard. Loud and clear." Engels chuckled, a throaty rumble that seemed to come from deep in his belly. "Like thunder, red man. They will hear my power like thunder. You Indians seem to believe so much in spirits. Well, I only hope for their sakes they see the spirit of death in my warning. It will be their last chance.

"There's something else, too, Indian, that I want you to think about. Your squaw." Engels's voice softened, a cold tone edged with lust and hate. "I will take your squaw. I will have her any way I desire. And you, fine warrior, broken and beaten at my hand, will watch every minute of it. Before I kill you. And her."

Running Elk lunged at Engels, his hands like claws as he went for the white man's throat.

Fear flickered through Engels's eyes.

A rifle butt chopped across the back of Running Elk's head, dropped him at the feet of Engels.

Viciously, Engels drove a kick across Running Elk's jaw, flipped the Indian on his back.

"Take him away," Engels snarled, his jowl quivering from rage. "The sight of him makes me sick."

Engels spun, spitting out orders to his men. "Get them moving on those crates. What are you doing standing there gaping at me for?" he rasped at Sunther and Stanley. "Get moving!"

The two hesitated, then wheeled and began heading out of the gorge.

"Mervin. I want your men spread out across these mountains. Double the guard. If it is Bolan, then we won't have to go to him. He'll come to us. And when he does, well, I want to greet the bastard properly.''

Engels stood unmoving as his men hastened to carry out his orders. Dark thoughts, worry, crept into his mind. Up to now everything had gone so damn smooth. All the right contacts. All the slaughter and treachery that had gotten him this far. All the key people right in his pocket.

Engels turned, watched his men drag the fallen Running Elk into the tunnel that led to the catacombs. Tombs. Sacred burial ground. Zuni. Navaho. Pueblo. Hopi. It didn't matter to Engels. The underground tunnels served their purpose for him. As everything and everyone else did.

The young Indian's words echoed in Engels's mind.

The warrior has come for your destruction . . .

Just what the hell was happening, the renegade operative wondered.

Had a devil from the past been resurrected?

Was that devil—Mack Bolan?

If it was, then Engels knew he would soon find out.

An icy chill tapped his spine.

The Executioner.

A one-man fighting force.

A devil that could rain hellfire and destroy Engels's master scheme before it ever got off the ground.

Engels cursed. The sound held a fearful ring that lingered in his ears.

Like a death knell.

7

The desert stretched away from Bolan like an endless brown sea.

Desolation.

A silent killer.

Mesas, canyons and jagged hill belts were the only features that broke this lunarlike landscape, added a haunting beauty to the flatness.

Within hours, Bolan knew, as he looked at the sun about to clear the mountain ridges to the east, the land would become a blazing caldron, capable of sucking the life juices right out of him.

There were three full canteens, packets of salt and plenty of food in the back of the Jimmy. Still, after years of living on the knife edge of disaster, the warrior knew that in the desert his survival could be threatened in the blink of an eye. And at the moment there were cannibals out there who could chew the life out of him faster than the sun could claim his life.

Bolan followed the tracks left by the assault truck, even though he'd long since lost sight of the vehicle, as if the desert had just swallowed it.

Yeah, the danger was definitely out there, some-where on this vast, parched hellhole, Bolan decided.

His blitzkrieg presence would be made known to Engels as soon as the blond lackey who had escaped Bolan's wrath returned to the hardsite. While Bolan hunted them, they would wait. Or come hunting for his head.

Then, let the war begin.

Fire and sword had come to this ancient, brutal land in the name of justice, in the being of Mack Bolan.

The scene of slaughter back at Gila Plains raised one very disturbing question in Bolan's mind.

Was John Travers dirty?

There was indeed something about the way in which the ex-Green Beret had handled the situation in town that struck Bolan as peculiar. Deadly, too. The Special Forces men whom Bolan had seen during combat duty in Vietnam as a sniper marksman were the best trained, toughest guerrilla fighters in the world. And John Travers was a fighting man, quite ready and able to jump into a hellzone, guns blazing.

Jamie had hinted to Bolan that the elder Travers just might be dirty.

And if the ex-Special Forces man was crooked, then Bolan knew he would soon show his true colors. Travers would have to—if he'd chosen sides. And if he had, then there would be no massive police manhunt.

Travers would simply run straight to Engels.

And the manhunt would become a death hunt.

The cold, callous voice Travers had used in warn-ing the woman about her interference still haunted

Bolan. The Executioner recognized the voice of desperation, the voice of guilt covering deception with anger.

Bolan also realized that his hellstorming arrival in the "dirty land" now put Jamie's life in jeopardy. If Travers suspected she knew something he would get it out of her. One way or another.

Things were heating up, the soldier told himself. The war was not yet full-scale, but the opening guns had sounded.

The desert floor began to rise under Bolan. He sent the Jimmy up a long, steady incline, drove a good two klicks before he came to the lip of a rise overlooking a valley. There, Bolan killed the engine. Grabbing his binoculars, he stepped from the Jimmy, found cover behind a boulder and began surveying the mesa-studded valley.

From his hilltop vantage point, Bolan watched the early morning activity that had begun in the Navaho village several hundred yards across the valley.

A dozen sheep, several goats and cattle, their ribs outlined beneath dust-caked hides, moved listlessly between and in front of dilapidated wooden huts and crumbled adobe ruins that lined the base of an imposing mesa. Navaho women, dressed in velveteen blouses and calico skirts, carried *pa'hos* of cornmeal, while other women worked with patient skill weaving striped blankets hung from looms.

Men hung strips of rabbit hide, or pulverized the dried strips with stone mauls. Children, their flesh a smooth, deep bronze, ran through the village, chasing each other or rousing the domestic animals from lethargy. A cornfield, stalks brown and withered, spread out to the north of the village.

Bolan spotted the lone, hunched shape of a man, high atop the mesa behind the village.

As he lowered the glasses, Bolan felt a warm breeze wash over him. The faintest trace of a smile touched his lips. These Navaho, he could see, were struggling to hold on to the ways of their ancestors. There was peace down there in the valley, in the way they lived. They had the freedom of people who had chosen to live as they wished.

Bolan brought the field glasses to his eyes again, searched the weathered, time-ravaged faces. There was strength, Bolan saw, etched into each face, a strength born from enduring years of hardship, a strength that came from deep within. To the casual observer, the land, their lives, seemed to have given them nothing. But Bolan knew that struggle in the face of hardship and suffering fed the spirit, made it stronger. Often, he thought, those who appeared to have nothing had everything.

This was a land, a people, Bolan knew, removed from modern time. The American frontier lived on, at least in spirit, in this wild, untamed, unforgiving land.

Yeah, if only the rat race of twentieth-century civilization could see this. The Executioner felt a great sadness well up inside of him. He realized that civilization had lost touch with the tranquillity that a simple, good life brought, had forgotten the heritage that made America great.

These Navaho, Bolan plainly saw, had suffered greatly, but they still refused to let the world define them; they had defined it. Defining the world was the first step that a warrior took in understanding the world. Pain and suffering encouraged the warrior to align the boundaries of the world, create the private and personal landscape of the heart, the soul. Hardship made a man dig inside of himself. Suffering put his ass on the chopping block. When all seemed lost, as Bolan had experienced time and again, only then did a man really begin to live. The endurance of hardship was a constant process of rebirth for the warrior.

Mack Bolan knew those Navaho understood this.

Suddenly, Bolan spotted a trail of dust, perhaps six hundred yards north, toward the rugged canyon country. The distance was too far for him to see clearly the figure on horseback. But something about the breakneck speed the rider demanded from his mount alerted Bolan to some unseen danger.

THEY FLEW WEST, the two JetRanger helicopters skimming the desert floor.

Aboard the lead strike copter, Sunther pressed himself against the open starboard door. He saw the mesa loom up through the Plexiglas windshield like some monster about to devour them. Beneath him, the ground rushed past, a brown haze, close, so dangerously close.

But that was just fine, Sunther told himself, as he felt the adrenaline surge through his veins. This strike was supposed to be lightning swift and thunder loud.

They would descend on the village like devils from the sky, he thought. Then he felt the light-headed sensation he always experienced just prior to these attacks. Hell, it should have been enough that the Indians had been warned to stay away from the compound. They hadn't obeyed. Some had died. And this air strike, Sunther knew, would be their last warning. Then, Engels would allow him to raze the whole stinking village.

The real thing.

Just as in Nam where he'd been a door gunner aboard a Huey UH-1H. The Flying Devils, they'd called themselves. He'd seen his M-60 chewing up Cong ambush sites along the Mekong Delta. Hooches swept away by miniguns. That had been the real thing. That had been life. The only life. Death raining from above.

But knowing that this was just another strike against the Navaho took some of the thrill out of the whole run for Sunther. The Indians were hanging tough, and he didn't like that. The red bastards, he cursed to himself. Damn, how he hated those Navaho. They were just like the Vietnamese, the Salvadoran and Honduran peasants he'd blown away. They always seemed so damned peaceful, just looking at him with that proud defiance in their eyes when they should have been groveling at his feet for their lives. Instead, they acted as if they were better than he, Sunther's mind raged on.

Well, he thought, we'll just see who's better.

Sunther felt his body draw rigid after an involuntary shudder. He was determined to strike terror into their hearts—and make sure that terror stayed this time.

The chopper rose, lifting its snout like a killer shark streaking for bone and blood, cleared a barren ridge.

A cold smile smeared Sunther's face as he watched Wilson squeeze into the door next to him.

Sunther lifted his assault rifle. This warning would definitely be their last one, he vowed to himself. He was sick and tired of fucking around.

The whir of the rotor blades grew deafeningly loud in his ears.

BOLAN SAW THE DUST boil along the mesa. For a moment he peered at the lone figure at the far edge of the flat-topped rock. The Indian just sat there, cross-legged, like a stone carving.

The throbbing of rotor blades reached Bolan's ears. Combat senses instantly locked into full alert. A moment later the two copters appeared as if they'd risen straight up from the rock itself.

Without warning, the JetRangers descended on the village. Four assault rifles began blistering the village with a terrible racket.

Dogs, sheep and cattle dropped, pulverized into the ground by hails of hot lead, slugs chewing up their bodies and turning them into emaciated blood-and-fur clods.

Giant sheets of dust swept over the fleeing villagers. Women hauled in children, ducked into huts.

Insane-sounding laughter rang out from the cockpits. The gunners yelled, screamed obscenities at the Navaho. Bullets punched through blankets. Pottery exploded.

Bolan bolted toward his vehicle. He was too far away from the deathbirds to get off a good, quick shot at the rotor couplings, but the rocket launcher would bring those assault choppers down.

The Executioner fisted the RPG-7, with rage burning through him over this senseless attack.

Suddenly the shooting stopped.

Bolan looked up. The lone rider he'd seen moments before reined in his mount. Bolan watched as the Navaho shouted at the choppers, pulling an arrow from his quiver. The Indian was a good two hundred yards away from the aircraft. But Bolan guessed that the arrow he shot was for effect, the Navaho hoping to draw the gunships away from his village.

The Indian whipped the black stallion around, began racing his bareback mount toward the rugged hill country.

Bolan hopped into the 4X4, fired up the engine. He saw the helicopters hover over the village for several seconds, as if the cannibals were trying to decide what to do.

They decided.

Furiously, Bolan sent his Jimmy bounding back down the rise. In the distance the gunships glided away from the village. He cursed, knowing they would overrun the Indian in a matter of moments.

To bring those assault choppers down, the Executioner knew he had to get close.

But close, Bolan feared, might not come soon enough.

"I DON'T WANT TO KILL HIM. Not yet!" Sunther told Wilson in a loud, angry voice as wind and the roar of rotor blades filled the cockpit. "Relay that message to Rankin," he ordered the pilot. "Tell him to fly north to the other side of those hills. Come back through the canyon. We'll box him in." Sunther laughed. "Our boy, Young Eagle, thinks he can lose us in that maze of rock. Yeah, well, we'll play his game. For now."

"What's the plan?" Wilson asked.

Sunther looked the man in the eye. "Throw his red ass into that snake pit, that's the plan. That'll tell those Injuns back there that we mean business. Right?"

Sunther looked toward the Indian, several hundred feet beyond and below him.

"Hover this bird!" he commanded the pilot. "Let's see if Young Eagle can fly." Sunther roared with laughter.

And cut loose with his assault rifle.

A line of slugs stitched the ground beside the galloping stallion.

Hunched low on his mount, his face pressed against the animal's neck, Thomas Young Eagle held on to the mane in desperation, but absorbed the bone-jarring ride, remembering that the stallion was only an extension of his own body. It was how his ancestors had ridden.

The whine of rotor blades filled his ears, one long deafening shriek. He saw the puffs of dust erupt where bullets struck the hard-packed soil. The white eyes soldiers, he cursed, were playing with him, trying to terrorize him as they had his people. Young Eagle made up his mind not to fall prey to them, like the hare to the hawk.

The Indian kicked at the stallion's flanks, demanding more speed. He wanted to draw the *beliganos* down the canyon. There, he could hide in an arroyo, climb to the top of one of the hills and strike them dead with his arrows.

He heard their shouts, their curses, almost on top of him. His blood boiled from the seething hatred he felt for his tormentors. They had stolen his sister, Golden Rainbow. They demanded that his people leave the land of his ancestors. The white eyes were treacherous, brutal men. Young Eagle had to slay them for their wrongdoing.

The young Navaho saw the other bird of death soar past him, vanish beyond the jagged peaks ahead. He was now less than a hundred yards from the mouth of the ravine.

Suddenly, the chopper dropped beside Young Eagle.

Instinctively, Young Eagle swung to the other side of the horse, protected from their fire behind the animal's belly.

"Die, you red bastard!" he heard the *beligano* scream against the steady burp of his weapon.

And Young Eagle heard the bullets thud like stone into the stallion's side, felt the blood spray across his face. He threw himself away from the animal.

With a grunt of pain, Young Eagle hit the ground on his side, rolling. He heard the terrible sound of hind legs snapping as his stallion toppled in death, and he felt grief.

Such a beautiful animal, he heard his mind cry. Such a terrible waste. *Curse their black souls!*

And still the gunner kept laughing, triggering his rifle.

Feeling his heart pulsing clear up to his temples, Young Eagle sprinted toward a boulder. Arrows jumped out of his quiver, the tips banging off the back of his head before they fell to the ground.

Bullets drilled into the ground behind the Indian, tracking his flight like a line of deadly killer bees.

Bow in hand, Young Eagle dived over the boulder. Slugs whined off stone, spitting chips off Young Eagle's back.

The Navaho brave darted from boulder to boulder, shielding himself from the rain of bullets as he slid down the face of the ravine wall.

Dust billowed in the mouth of the narrow ravine where the JetRanger hovered.

Young Eagle turned, saw the white eyes in the doorway of the chopper point toward him.

Slowly, the JetRanger moved into the ravine like some monstrous predatory insect.

Young Eagle found the gully that had been cut by the summer thunderstorms. It was a steep climb, perhaps a hundred feet to the top. And when he reached the hill's summit, he would shoot his arrows, straight and sure, into the white demons who he knew would follow his ascent, searching for him.

As Young Eagle moved swiftly up the gully, he listened to the whirring rotors. Believing he was completely hidden for the moment behind the wall of rock, he climbed the gully with confidence.

But, as Young Eagle topped the gully, weapons suddenly opened up on him. Lead zinged all around him, created a gauntlet of certain death.

There was a lull in the shooting as Sunther and Wilson rammed home fresh clips.

Scrambling to his feet, Young Eagle charged toward a line of boulders.

The chopper rose above, behind Young Eagle.

Sunther and Wilson sprayed the area around the Navaho, forced him to turn away from the boulders. Yelling obscenities and threats, the two gunners followed the Indian's zigzagging run with twin lines of raking fire.

Young Eagle cried out in fear and surprise as he tripped, fell flat on his face. He looked up and saw the dust swirling all around him, near his face.

Their expressions twisted with murderous intent, Sunther and Wilson hosed the ground in front of Young Eagle with long bursts, inching their fire toward him.

A roar filled Young Eagle's ears. As the line of fire swept toward him, panic seized the Navaho. He rolled away, leaped to his feet but then fell again. He shot his hand out to grab the edge of the fissure, to clutch at anything.

He wondered why the white eyes stopped shooting, then realized he was momentarily out of their sight as he dangled from the edge.

Dust clogged Young Eagle's nose and throat from the whirlpool of dirt that the shrieking rotors kicked up. He dug his hands like claws into the lip, but felt his fingers sliding away from the fissure's edge. He twisted around and froze as he stared down at the fate that awaited him. His hearing, sharpened by his heightened terror, caught the sound of death.

Painful, horrible death.

Below Young Eagle, a den of rattlesnakes slithered over scattered human skulls and bones.

Waiting.

8

Bolan gunned the Jimmy into the ravine. Bearing down on the strike chopper, he saw the two door gunners swing their rifles toward him.

The Executioner stomped on the brakes, whipping his vehicle around to a dust-churning halt.

The curse that Sunther snarled, as he rammed another clip into his HK-91, was the last oath he ever uttered.

Death ended a treacherous existence that had been filled with senseless rage, unfounded fear and bitter frustration.

Bolan was out of the Jimmy, the mini-Uzi leaping up in his fist and barking out lethal messages, a millisecond before return fire ripped into his vehicle's hood.

Dust and noise swept over the Executioner as he crouched behind the left front fender of the vehicle.

Little Lightning spit out all its 20-round 9 mm projectiles, stitching the two door gunners. Both cannibals collided into each other. Blood and gore and shredded cloth sprayed the cockpit. Sunther's skull cracked off the edge of the frame. He fell from the open doorway, did a swan dive that ended when his body broke like a pretzel over a boulder.

The pilot hit the cyclic pitch stick in a desperate attempt to get the hell out of there. Panic showed on his face, and in his terror-stricken state he spun the copter's nose around, toward the hellstormer on the floor of the ravine.

It was a mistake that cost the flier his life.

Bolan slammed home a fresh clip into the Uzi's magazine, hosed the Plexiglas, unloading all twenty life-sucking rounds. Parabellum slugs punched through the windshield. Glass cracked, spiderwebbed in front of a face being blown away by the Executioner's furious assault.

Bolan saw the pilot's head disintegrate in chunks, blood splashing the instrument panel and the mangled windshield. As the pilot slumped forward, the unmanned copter spiraled crazily down and across the ravine.

Aware that the other strike chopper was out there, Bolan grabbed the Russian rocket launcher from the jeep. He ran toward the gully an instant before the out-of-control helicopter hammered into the wall of rock.

A thunderous explosion erupted. Shock waves pounded Bolan. A giant fireball whooshed across the ravine, debris banging off rock, razoring through the air.

Twisted, flaming wreckage crashed to the floor of the ravine.

The Executioner didn't look back.

YOUNG EAGLE HEARD A CRY of disbelief echo in his mind. He couldn't believe he was going to meet his end, broken and bloodied in a pit of vipers, his flesh the food for serpents. Terror paralyzed him. A plea for help caught in his parched throat, strangled him.

There was no help. There was no way out but down.

The *beliganos* had won. Their viper pit would consume him. And his people, he knew now for certain, would die by the hands of the white eyes soldiers. He cursed them, cursed his own recklessness at having forgotten in his haste to take vengeance that the pit of snakes had been put there by the soldiers to send others to their deaths.

He felt the dirt and stones beneath his hands dig into his flesh like ground glass. His weight kept dragging him down, a fraction of an inch at a time, pulling him away from the edge.

Horror then became shock when Young Eagle felt his hands finally slip off the edge.

But a strange sense of disembodiment filled the Indian, made him feel as if he floated on air.

Was this how death felt, he wondered, as the pit seemed to shoot up at him. Then, as if lightning had struck, there was a terrible wrenching pain in his arms and shoulders, and the sky appeared to drop down on his face.

Dust filled Young Eagle's nose and throat, gagging him as his face slammed into the hard-packed soil. His breathing sharp in his ears, he stared at the ground beneath him for long moments, waiting to feel the fangs spear into his flesh.

But nothing happened.

Finally, he dared to look up.

And Young Eagle saw a white man with a formidable-looking weapon looming over him. He stared up at the white man's face, a face unlike any visage he'd ever seen. Eyes like chips of ice stared down at him. It seemed as if those eyes pierced right through him, into his very being.

All of a sudden, Young Eagle felt no fear as he peered at the white man's face, searched deeply into those icy blue eyes. Yes, he thought, there was courage, great courage in those eyes, the courage of a man at war with all that was evil under the sun.

And there was something else in those eyes, too.

Compassion. Wisdom.

Young Eagle had seen the face of a warrior on only one other man. Heart Sun. The ancient chief of his village.

Slowly, Young Eagle stood. He heard Heart Sun's voice filtering into his mind, and Young Eagle recalled the prophecy.

"You are he?"

"He who?" Bolan asked.

"You are the great white warrior Heart Sun has said would come and take war to the soldiers of the mountain." He paused. "You can be no other. I have heard the thunder. I have seen the fire in the sky."

Bolan looked up, and the young Navaho followed his gaze.

The backup strike chopper soared over the peaks far to the north.

"Well, I'm going to be the great white nothing if those guys have anything to say about it. Get behind the rocks," Bolan told Young Eagle. He lifted the RPG-7 and ran toward the edge of the hill.

"You are he," Young Eagle said, astonished and suddenly filled with pride and wonder.

Young Eagle crouched behind the boulders, watched as the tall white warrior dropped down into the gully, knelt behind the rocks for cover.

The gunship swooped down into the ravine.

Bolan lifted the tube over the edge, waited.

The assault chopper closed down on the Executioner's position.

The whir of rotor blades grew to a frenzied shriek in Young Eagle's ears. He saw one of the soldiers point toward the warrior. Their rifles opened up without warning.

The Executioner lined up the RPG's sights, zeroed them on the fuselage.

The deathbird descended from the sky, toward Bolan.

Hot lead ricocheted off rock near Bolan, spitting chips of stone dangerously close to his face.

He steadied his aim, locked in the sights with powerful arms, corded with muscle.

"Come on, you bastards," he rasped through gritted teeth, and squeezed the trigger.

The rocket-propelled grenade whooshed away, trailing yellow flame.

A gunner screamed something.

The strike copter vanished inside a brilliant orange fireball.

Jumping to his feet, Young Eagle almost shouted in joy as he watched the fiery hull, the death bird of the white eyes, plummet into the ravine.

Bolan turned and walked back toward the Navaho.

"What's your name?" the Executioner inquired.

"I am called Young Eagle," the Indian said, drawing a deep breath, squaring his shoulders.

"And I'm Bolan," the Executioner said. "Young Eagle, you were right when you said I'm here to bring war to the soldiers of the mountain. But if I'm going to help you and your village, I need to know everything about these men. All right?"

"You ask me questions, Warrior Bolan. I will answer."

Bolan glanced at the snake pit. "Is this the work of those men?"

"Yes. To silence the tongues of those who have seen their evil, they throw many Navaho and Mexicans to the snakes. White man, too. The white eyes leader, he is one evil man. They come from the sky, many moons ago, to the mountains where the spirits of the Pueblo dwell. They build huts there. They bring in guns and many armed soldiers by the great birds. I have seen it. Many times.

"They come to the village, lure some of the weaker ones away with promises of gold. Make my brothers work like slaves. Then they kill them. No reason. Just kill. They are bad white eyes with black hearts. They tell us to leave, or they say they will kill us all. They came to the village at night and stole my sister, Golden Rainbow." Vengeance burned in his dark eyes. "I will go to the mountain myself. I will free her. I will kill the white devils with my own hands!"

Bolan held the rocket launcher low by his side, fixed a steady gaze on the young Navaho. "Let's get back to your village," he said, turning away from the Indian. "When they find what's left of their buddies down there, they'll come back. And this time they'll be playing for keeps."

Young Eagle hesitated, watched as the warrior disappeared down the gully.

"Wait. I will come with you. I will fight the white devils beside you!"

On their way back to the Jimmy, Bolan learned more about Engels's operation from Young Eagle. He also discovered the reason for his peculiar speech, his accent, the almost poetic way he talked. He, like others of this rebel band, wished to live in the old ways, spoke only Navaho among themselves, and when speaking English, tried to match their own idiom as closely as possible. Bolan had the eerie feeling that he was caught in a time warp, living one hundred and fifty years before, when the Navaho fought their cousins, the Apache.

The young Indian, whom Bolan guessed to be in his early twenties, told Bolan that he had counted more than two dozen soldiers guarding the perimeter of the mountain hardsite. But Young Eagle went on to say that he had done his reconnoitering at night, and had not gotten close enough to the compound to be certain about their numbers.

During two of his hunts for rabbit and water, Young Eagle had seen a very large plane land on the airstrip that the soldiers had forced the Navaho and Mexicans to clear. A dozen more armed, brown-uniformed soldiers disembarked from that plane, and crates were hauled from out of the hull.

A cargo plane, Bolan figured. If Engels's operation was as big as Bolan suspected, then the renegade operative certainly had connections around the globe. There were cannibals on the other end of Engels's Thailand pipeline, who supplied the Company traitor. Khmer Rouge rebels, Bolan suspected. Some of the dirtiest, ugliest cutthroat bastards in all of war-torn and troubled Southeast Asia.

Bolan knew that as a PM Engels had had plenty of opportunities over the years to search out the suppliers of arms and the dealers in heroin on the international black market. Just how far the tentacles of this particular hydra now reached Bolan would have to uncover during deep penetration into the hardsite. If there was indeed a major arms-opium deal going down sometime in the near future, as the rat-faced Kiley told Bolan before Big Thunder had blown the punk's head off, then Bolan figured a number of very key players would be at that scene.

One carefully planned and swiftly executed strike by the Executioner could turn that scene into their deathbed. And bite out quite a large chunk of Engels's arms-opium pipeline.

Bolan couldn't help but wonder how many people, good and bad, had died because of Engels's treachery and brutality. And the Executioner's gut feeling told him that Engels was playing for something bigger, something far more deadly that Bolan had yet to discover.

Young Eagle went on to tell Bolan that the soldiers had a tremendous weapon, hidden behind boulders near the airstrip, quite capable, he believed, of blowing any aircraft out of the sky.

Flames crackled and thick clouds of oily smoke rose from the ruins of the downed aircraft behind Bolan and Young Eagle as they moved up beside the jeep.

"Can you describe this weapon?" the Executioner asked.

"It is a cannon. A very big cannon."

A howitzer, Bolan decided. With an operation like Engels was running and, by all accounts, given Engels's bloodthirsty nature, Bolan knew the man would have no qualms about blowing a search helicopter or any civilian or military aircraft out of the sky if he felt threatened. If Engels was reckless or insane enough to call immediate attention from the law to this remote region of desert that he seemed to own, thus endangering his whole operation, then it told Bolan that either the man was desperate and felt he had nothing to lose or he believed his pot of gold was just within his grasp.

Bolan assumed both. And he assumed the worst.

"Warrior Bolan," Young Eagle said in a solemn voice.

The Executioner stopped beside the jeep, met the Navaho's gaze.

"We are proud people, the Navaho. Chief Heart Sun led us away from the white man's reservation, from the white man's prison, so that we might have a chance to live again in the spirit of our ancestors. We cannot be the warriors...we cannot be the raiders my ancestors were. That would mean death to us. Still, we carry the heart of the warrior. Heart Sun tells me many stories of battle when he was a great warrior and raider in his youth.

"Many years he fought the Apache dogs. Many he killed. Many years it took Heart Sun and his village to settle the land. Heart Sun teaches me that water is life. For any who make the desert home. The water of life makes itself known only to the warrior. The land is a gift from the Great Spirit. If a warrior knows how to live with the land, then the earth feeds him.

"And we will not leave this land. We will stand and fight. We will die before we return to the reservation. The great chief has said we must not live in fear of the white eyes and the dead anymore. Yes, there is death now around us. But you, Warrior Bolan, are the one who comes from death to bring life to all who deserve.

"The white eyes of the mountain, they think we are weak, and stupid, and foolish. They use the Navaho for his strength, then kill him. This is wrong. This cannot go unpunished."

Bolan read the defiant hatred in Young Eagle's eyes, heard in his voice a grim determination to take vengeance into his own hands. It was something Bolan understood all too well, and he agreed with the young Navaho that Engels and his cannibals should not go unpunished. But Bolan felt that Young Eagle could somehow become a liability to his mission when the numbers began to tumble. Young Eagle was too stubborn and reckless for his own good. Emotion often clouded judgment. The Indian's raw hatred had blinded him to his own safety.

There were no dead horses in Mack Bolan's mind.

Bolan saw trouble ahead with Young Eagle.

"What is the matter, Warrior Bolan?" Young Eagle asked. "You are silent. Do you doubt my words? Do you doubt my skill as a warrior?"

"No, I don't doubt either your words or your skill, Young Eagle," Bolan answered. "I just don't want to see you get your head blown off before you've grown into your warrior skin."

Bolan opened the door, hopped into the Jimmy.

With a puzzled expression, Young Eagle stood utterly still for several seconds. Then he nodded and moved around to the passenger side of the 4X4.

Bolan fired up the engine. Glancing into the sideview mirror, he saw the flames dance from the blackened hulls behind him.

Death by fire.

Death by sword.

Something told Mack Bolan the worst was yet to come.

Hellfire had only begun to rain down on the dirty land.

9

At first glance, Bolan thought the Navaho village had been abandoned. Then he saw a figure—whom he guessed to be the chief—sitting cross-legged in front of his ceremonial hogan at the base of the mesa.

The death and devastation that the strike helicopters had wreaked had not touched the villagers themselves. The pulpy and bloody remains of dogs, goats, sheep and cattle were strewed around the village. Swarms of flies crawled over the bloated carcasses.

Fragments of pottery crunched beneath the Jimmy's wheels. Bullet-shredded blankets hung in tatters from looms. In the sky above the village, a dozen buzzards hovered like an ominous black cloud.

Bolan and Young Eagle stepped out of the jeep.

The Executioner noticed, indeed felt the eerie stillness that hung like a shroud about the village.

Heart Sun just gazed up at the lone white man.

Bolan thought that the Navaho chief looked as old and weathered as the surrounding landscape. Carefully, Bolan searched the old Indian's face, saw, and sensed in Heart Sun's silence, great strength and courage. His was a face that commanded Bolan's attention.

And respect.

A face, Bolan decided, shaped by a very long and very hard life. A soul baptized by the blood of war, strengthened through terrible hardship.

The silence thickened.

Bolan looked up, spotted the scavengers of death circling directly overhead.

Heart Sun's sun-cracked lips parted. He raised his head a little. His stare didn't waver off the white man. "I have heard the thunder. I have seen the fire from my hill. I have smelled death in the morning, as have the vultures. Tell me, white man. Who are you?"

"He's the one you have spoken of, Heart Sun," Young Eagle anxiously informed the chief. "I have seen him shoot down the birds of death."

"Be silent, Young Eagle. This is not your place to speak," Heart Sun said, his voice calm somehow, even in reproach.

Embarrassed, Young Eagle turned his gaze away from the chief.

Bolan and Heart Sun looked at each other for a long moment.

"My name is Mack Bolan, Heart Sun. I've come here to destroy the men who've been terrorizing you and your people. They've killed many men, your people and mine."

"Are you ... from the government?"

"No."

"You are a warrior, that much I can see. If you do not fight for your government, then for whom do you fight?"

"I fight for no one man," Bolan told the chief. "I fight for every man. So that all good men can live."

Heart Sun bowed his head in a shallow nod. "I see. I understand. And I know now who you are."

Peering at Heart Sun, Bolan wondered just what the chief meant by his cryptic words, but dismissed them from his mind.

"Chief Heart Sun," Bolan said, "I think it's urgent we move your people somewhere else, far away from here. At least for now. The men I'm hunting will come back here when they find out I've killed some of their numbers."

Heart Sun shook his head. "These men, they will not find their dead anytime soon. My village is safe for this day and perhaps tomorrow. It is something I sense. There is no danger from them at this time. I know these soldiers. They are cowards. They are evil men. They strike only when it is to their advantage, when they are safe in their numbers. Then they kill for no reason. But evil needs no reason. Evil kills because it is what evil wants.

"You and I know this. And as a warrior, I have seen evil in my life. I have warred against the forces of light and dark that control the universe. And I understand these forces that pull the living and the dead together. No. We are not in any immediate danger from the men you must hunt and kill. You are the living. They are the dead. They wait for your judgment."

Bolan didn't know much about Navaho witchcraft and mysticism, but he could sense that Heart Sun was a wise and spiritual man. And a man as old as Heart Sun obviously didn't get to such an age by not dealing with and coming to some understanding about the "forces of light and dark." Heart Sun was, after all, a part of history, an Indian warrior, chief and shaman who had lived and fought in a time Bolan had only read about in history books.

Heart Sun was history.

And Mack Bolan realized that he had a chance now to experience a part of history that had built and shaped what was present-day America, for better or worse.

Heart Sun rose to his feet, a movement so effortless that the casual observer wouldn't have noticed the chief even moved.

"You would do me a great honor, Bolan, if you would join me for a meal. I have waited years since my first vision, a vision of all that is about to pass. There is a reason why we are here now, why the Great Spirit has not yet taken me. Yes, there is much we have to talk about. Before the final battle."

Bolan felt an urgent need to get on with his desert search and destroy. But how could he decline hospitality from a man who had lived his entire life as a warrior? How could he say no to such a humble offer from a man as great as Heart Sun, no matter how important Bolan's mission?

Engels could wait for the moment, Bolan finally decided. History couldn't.

Besides, as long as he was in the village, near the Navaho, then there was no way Engels and his cut-throat savages would strike again.

And meet with any success.

Bolan felt a kinship growing between himself and Heart Sun. Something inside Bolan told him to not let this moment pass.

"I accept, Heart Sun," Bolan said. "And it's you who do me the honor."

Heart Sun searched Bolan's face for a moment, as if trying to see into his soul. "Young Eagle. Bring us something to eat."

Heart Sun turned, and Bolan followed the chief toward his hogan.

Bolan and Heart Sun sat cross-legged on the dirt floor of the chief's hogan. Between the Executioner and the chief was a sand painting. Prayer sticks and masks, which Heart Sun used in ceremonies, leaned against the wall, darkened by shadow.

Young Eagle gave Bolan and the chief each a bowl of cornmeal, then moved to the far corner. There, he sat in respectful silence.

The two men ate for several moments before the chief spoke.

"I have told the others to stay inside their hogans. There has been great fear in the village. Many are old, and they remember cruel times of violence and death such as this. Some are sick, and they lack the faith that will make them well. When I led them away from the reservation years ago I did not promise them it would be easy. We have rejected the ways of a people who invaded our land, a people, I still believe, who enslaved us. I feel no hatred or bitterness toward the white man. And you will understand why in a moment.

"Some of the others, they cannot understand this, because they remember better days. We still hold on to Navaho teaching and tradition, but is it not better to change in some small ways than to die altogether?

"I am the only survivor of the Long Walk forced upon us by Carson. When winter came in the year of the Long Walk, the white eyes soldiers had destroyed all of our grain. We lived on piñon nuts, or we would have starved. Some of my brothers were naked in the cold. And many died. I was but a boy at that time, and it was a great test of my strength. A warrior, as you know, is always tested. The only way he gains power is through the test.

"My search for power has shown me that I could not completely forget the old ways. My brothers, they understood power, they understood the test. Power is not understood today by many young Indians who live on the reservation, who live like the white man. And it shows. In reservations across this land it is something that is killing him, his spirit. He cannot accept the change. He cannot accept that he had been conquered, not by the white man, but by his own destiny. And those who conquer always grow fat and content because of their triumph. Those who appear so strong in their victory will grow weaker by the day. And they, in turn, will be conquered.

"It is happening now. I can feel it around me. It wearies and frightens your people into despair. They were destroyers, many of the white men. And no destroyer of anything that is good can be allowed to live. No taker is allowed to live on to keep serving himself. The tyrant grows weak and falls prey to another tyrant."

Bolan looked deep into the black, watery pools that were Heart Sun's eyes. Give or take ten years, Bolan figured Heart Sun was pushing 130. Heart Sun did indeed look ancient, Bolan decided. But he had seen the man move with a grace and ease that a man eighty years younger would have envied. And the voice was still steady, strong with conviction.

Still, it was Heart Sun's eyes that made Bolan wonder most about the man. They were like mirrors to his soul, holding all the pain and suffering, all the triumph and bitter defeat he'd seen. They were eyes that had searched for all that was good and bad in men, and had seen that good and bad.

Bolan knew he was in the presence of a warrior like himself, a man who had walked many terrible miles through hellfire.

"On our way through the Tunicha and Zuni Mountains to Sumner," Heart Sun continued, "the young walked while the old and sick rode in wagons. Many died. Some were stolen away into slavery by whites and Mexicans. It took a long time, what seemed like an eternity to a young boy, before we reached the place the whites had chosen for us.

"For some time I watched my brothers and sisters suffer, live like dogs on this place along the Pecos. To make our suffering and humiliation worse, the soldiers had thrown us in with the Apache. I can remember it all as if it was only yesterday. Almost no food. The Apache dogs raiding our camps. The river running over and destroying our irrigation ditches. Having to live in holes in the ground like rats when the wind blew our shelters away. All the time I dreamed of canyons, and mountains, and open desert plains. Hoping to return. Wanting to escape the trap that had become our lives.

"Finally, the whites saw their failure. We were allowed to return to our homeland.

"I tell you this only because I sense we are alike in many ways, Bolan. Our spirits are the same. We have seen and known many of these same things. War. Suffering. Death. Vengeance. I see it in your eyes. I feel it in your presence. Even in the silence, we understand each other."

Bolan felt a strange heat coming from the chief's body, experienced some sudden surge of power. He kept his gaze fixed on Heart Sun, listening.

"I tell you about these things because you are a warrior, created and tested by forces beyond mere sight and sound. These forces have brought you here. And they are at work this very minute, seeking to destroy you. The forces of darkness, they never sleep.

"I tell you about the Long Walk because as a warrior, a man who seeks power, you can see that nothing ever really changes. The suffering the red man has endured has changed nothing in the end. I have often wondered if this civilization was worth the defeat of the Indian. Has anything become better? Which world is more civilized? The old world of the red man? Or the world created in the name of civilization by the white man after our fall?''

Bolan picked up on the sound of calm detachment in Heart Sun's voice. And the Executioner knew that Heart Sun didn't expect any answers from him. The past had been created, and in the present, no man, red or white, could be held accountable for history, nor could he answer for the atrocities committed by both the Indians and the whites during the fierce fighting that had eventually settled the West.

But then again, Bolan wondered, just what had been settled? And how much better was the world now because of what had happened between the Indian and the European settlers?

Was mankind then, Bolan wondered, doomed to fulfill some horrible and tragic destiny it was unable to avoid?

Bolan had a gut feeling that Heart Sun's words were leading up to something like the thoughts he now had.

"As a boy I had my first vision. In it I saw the coming of Carson and his soldiers, the Long Walk my people would suffer. I described mountains and canyons I had never seen. I named names of many in my tribe who would not reach Sumner. The elders believed I was delirious with fever when I said these things. They said I spoke in a voice that was not mine, but I cannot remember. 'How can it be,' they said, 'he is only a boy, not yet six summers old. He knows nothing of these places, these men. Do the evil spirits live in him?'

"Then, all I had seen came to pass, and there were many who were astonished and frightened. Since, I have seen many dreams come to pass. And in my final years I have seen the death of the white eyes.''

Bolan saw Heart Sun's gaze shift away from him. A distant, haunted look filled the Navaho's eyes.

Young Eagle sat up straight, his eyes wide.

"It is the most terrible vision yet. There is the sound of thunder rolling, like the rage of some beast across the sky, a noise so loud, so awesome the very earth trembles beneath my feet. The sky is black, and seems to sit right on top of me, a blackness that lives, that breathes an air filled with sulfur. Then I am blinded by the flashes of great clouds of fire. Blood pours over my head and it burns my flesh like fire. There are screams of men in horrible pain, but I can sense their evil, and I know they deserve this death. They cry out in tongues I have never heard. There is more fire. More burning blood. More raging thunder.

"And then, I am alone with death. There is silence. The new dawn nears.

"The sun, red like blood, rises behind me. Ashes reach out to me, from nowhere, yet everywhere. The voice booms like cannon fire and says, 'You have won the final victory. Your heart may rest at last.' And darkness comes once more."

Bolan sat in rapt attention. From out of the murky light, Heart Sun's voice seemed to come from a great distance, but still Bolan heard the voice as if the chief spoke into his ears.

"There is one last cloud of fire, and this cloud is the biggest and most terrible yet. The cloud sweeps over me, but it doesn't burn as the others did. For a moment I am blinded by a light so dazzling it makes the sun appear pale and weak. Then, as my sight slowly returns, I see a man, a white man in the distance. He steps out of the darkness. He is cut and bloodied from a fierce battle. He has death in his eyes. He has death on his face. I sense that he carries great pain and suffering in his heart, but I know he has tasted many victories over death. He has conquered, but most important, he has conquered himself.

"I look into his eyes, and he is gone. Like smoke. Like a ghost."

Bolan felt a coldness settle over him as he gazed into Heart Sun's dark eyes.

"Those eyes, that face," he told Bolan. "I am certain. They belong to you."

Hard silence.

Bolan thought he heard a wind sigh outside. He sat speechless. He felt numb for some reason, drained. Bolan read into the stone-cold look in Heart Sun's eyes, and he knew now beyond the shadow of a doubt that the chief had indeed seen that vision.

Many times.

And Heart Sun believed.

"In my vision, it is not clear whether you live... or die."

Heart Sun sounded genuinely saddened by what he told Bolan.

"There is a place. There I have done battle with the Apache, the butchers who killed my family when I was in my youth. This place is where I avenged my kin. And this place is where their spirits dwell. It is sacred ground. It is only there that I might be able to learn more about the outcome of this final battle. There are weapons, buried deep in the tunnels. You must go there with me. For your own life. And for the deliverance of my people. You, Bolan, may be faced with your greatest test yet. You will need all of your power."

Damn, Bolan thought. He had to get back out there in the desert, find and destroy Engels and his cannibals. The Executioner had started a war, and he knew he had to end it soon, or it might end him.

Still, he felt great respect for Heart Sun.

What if something Heart Sun showed or told him did, in fact, determine the outcome of his search and destroy, Bolan wondered. Or even determined some part of it.

He decided against going to the place of power that Heart Sun spoke about. The Executioner knew he didn't have any time to spare.

"Heart Sun," Bolan began, "you are a wise man and a great warrior. I, too, can sense these things. I, too, understand something about the forces of light and dark. And, as you said, those forces are at work right this minute. They are out there. And they mean you great harm.

"There are many things, I believe, that I could learn from you. But you, your people and many others are in danger until I finish what I came here to do. I have to find these men. I have to see their base in the daylight. I have to use the cover of night to penetrate their defense and kill them. Surely you understand that I need this time to plan my attack."

Heart Sun looked steadily at Bolan for a long moment. Then he nodded that he understood.

"Only you," the chief said, "know what you must do. Will you return?"

"Before the sun sets. I hope you'll rethink what I said about leaving here. How far is this place of power from here?"

"Perhaps a half day's journey. West."

"On foot?" Bolan asked.

"Yes," Heart Sun answered.

Bolan stood. "Would you consider leaving tonight?"

Heart Sun looked up at Bolan. "When you return we will discuss what you have seen. Yes, I will think about taking my people away from here."

"I can take you to the mountain," Young Eagle suggested.

"No," Bolan answered. "I have to do this alone, Young Eagle. Too many good people have died out here already."

"Yes, but my sister..."

"Young Eagle, you are a stubborn and rebellious one," Heart Sun scolded. "You will stay here with me. Bolan does not need you tripping all over his feet."

Young Eagle seemed to shrink back into the shadows, a look of disappointment on his face.

"Besides," Heart Sun said, "when Bolan returns he will need you to lead him to my place on the rock." Heart Sun returned his attention to Bolan. "There we will share the silence. The night will come. You will go from there into battle."

Bolan stared at Heart Sun's time-worn, pain-punished features. Yeah, Bolan thought, Heart Sun had known more trouble than any one man had a right to know.

And it was at that moment that Mack Bolan vowed to himself that Heart Sun and his people would suffer no more at the hands of Engels's men.

Bolan spoke to Young Eagle. "You'll get your sister back. Safe. I promise. The others, too."

Bolan left the hogan.

If anything happened to the Navaho while he was gone, then the Executioner knew the renegade operatives would not meet an easy end.

They would die.

Hard.

Very hard.

10

Armando Salviche was sick and tired of standing around with his hands jammed into the pant pockets of his Yves Saint-Laurent suit. Salviche had already been there with Damien Bozzarelli and their combined muscle for more than a day, and still no smack. Didn't Engels know Salviche and Bozzarelli and the boys were no small-timers? They sure as hell didn't need to be wasting their valuable time in some armpit of the world, watching Engels and his hard guys strutting around like peacocks, snapping out orders at big-time, megabuck-making drug kings.

Just what the hell was this? Salviche swore viciously to himself.

Shit, the druglord thought, one fat pinkie skillfully picking at the inside of a cocaine-inflamed nostril. He wondered why these CIA hotshots didn't have any respect? Hell, Salviche swore, he made it the hard way. Scratching. Clawing. Kicking ass over half of New York. He hit pay dirt, and here he was, top dog, waiting, sweating his ass off and ruining a three-hundred-dollar suit. Damn, he should be back in Manhattan even now. In fact, he better be back there by tonight.

With about a dozen fat white liners laid out in front of him.

"Hey, Armando. Snap out of it. What you doing—daydreaming?"

Salviche looked across the large, Spartan room at John Engels. Hotshot CIA killer, the druglord thought. Such a hotshot he's gotta hide out in no-man's-land and surround himself with a bunch of crazy gringo *cabrones* who can't show their stinking selves in the real world, either. He wished he could pull his piece and waste them all right there. That goddamn smack belonged to him.

Again, Salviche glanced around the CIA quarters. The short, stocky Bozzarelli sat next to Salviche. The Italian druglord appeared very nervous, and Salviche could understand that. Bozzarelli had a deadly fear of snakes, and as if to taunt or perhaps feed Bozzarelli's paranoia, Engels had four large glass cages filled with the biggest, fattest rattlesnakes Salviche had ever seen.

Spartan furnishings, sure, Salviche thought sarcastically, if you didn't mind sleeping in a den of vipers.

It was crazy, he told himself. So damn crazy. They were all crazy!

Salviche and Bozzarelli had each brought along four gunmen just in case pure mean crazy turned into all hell breaking loose. Salviche had heard about Mara-quez and Diablo down in Miami—the poor, stinking slobs. He'd met the two several times, running with them up and down the East Coast, searching out hustlers, creating, then working their own pipeline.

But Maraquez and Diablo had gotten greedy. Salviche always knew he couldn't trust those two out of his sight. Besides, he thought, they were just hard to work with, bitching about this, whining about that. To top it off, they were pigs. And like pigs, they had gotten fat, and worse, gotten caught, been ready to squeal to the Feds about the pipeline. But instead of finding two punks ready to drag down everybody, and that included himself, Salviche realized, what the Feds found were two wide-eyed, deaf, dumb and blind pigs. Deaf, dumb and blind because Engels's men, Salviche could swear even though he could not prove, had drilled a bullet at close range through their foreheads.

How the killers had gotten past the jail guards and terminated Maraquez and Diablo was a mystery to Salviche. But, he knew, that was how those CIA guys were. They were like ghosts. Shadows. They had no souls. Either whoever had done that job was very good at what he did, or someone's palm had gotten greased with some fat green. It was the latter that Salviche wanted to believe.

As Salviche looked at the dozen soldiers lounging around Engels's quarters, he realized that any one of those men was capable of assassinating a target, then vanishing from the killzone like some phantom. The druglord tried to force some bravado he couldn't find inside, no matter how hard he searched himself, hoping he looked as cold and steely-eyed as those gringo pigs.

And they just sat or stood there, arms draped over the edges of the snake cages, watching Salviche.

Salviche shivered, wondering if they could read his mind. The druglord squared his shoulders, reminding himself to stand big. After all, he was rich and powerful. And after this shipment, he wouldn't need these crazy gringos anymore.

Salviche turned his attention to Engels, wondered then just how long he'd been standing there in silence. This Engels, the man who loved his snakes, was the craziest of them all, Salviche thought. The bastard talked about killing as if it was something like preparing and eating a meal.

Then it dawned on Salviche that this was exactly how a man like Engels would see murder. Plan the victim's death like a gourmet meal, gourmet if the target was big-time—perhaps, Salviche thought, big-time like himself—then strike, slay the victim as if that target was food to be devoured and digested to sate the blood lust.

The thought sent a chill down Salviche's spine.

"Come on over here, Armando," Engels said. "You've been pacing around here all day, dying to sample this junk. Now's your chance."

The small crate was open. Salviche stared at the bricks of scag, neatly packaged in polyethylene bags. Uncut. Pure. He knew he was looking at millions in cash. Grown in the hot, hill country of the Golden Triangle.

A tribesman might walk a whole week, hauling as much as twenty-five kilos before he dumped the raw opium in a Thai border village. And, Salviche thought, the stupid, indigent primate would collect maybe twelve dollars for his trouble. That was only if the warlord was feeling particularly gracious that day. And twelve dollars would be perhaps the tribesman's only income for the whole year.

Engels, Salviche recalled, had once told him all this, a very long time ago. A time Salviche didn't want to remember. A time when he was scrubbing out toilets in a flophouse, or hustling whores along Times Square and Broadway.

Engels held up the crate's lid. "Go ahead, amigo. Take one of these bricks out and taste the stuff."

The dark-skinned Salviche looked at Engels for a second, returned the crazy killer's smile.

"I don't think I want this shipment stepped on. I think you understand this, amigo," Salviche said. "I am a businessman now, hey, and I have certain, uh, clients who have very high standards. Armando Salviche and our good amigo, Damien," he continued, turning and holding his hand out toward the other druglord, "have worked very hard for you over the years. We started out with nothing. We have since built a considerable empire. For us, and for you. I think, then, that it is only right and fair that we ask for a bigger percentage. No?"

Engels nodded slowly and smiled. He thumped Salviche on the back. "How right you are, Armando. You've worked very hard, as you say. And you've done a hell of a job. From what I hear. I say this to you and to Bozzarelli, here and now, in front of my men and yours." Engels smiled again. "Hey, I think it's fair, too. Whatever you want."

Salviche heard one of Engels's men chuckle softly behind him, but he ignored the man. Salviche's mind went over several ways he would like to kill Engels. He was determined to leave this hellhole with all of that smack.

Salviche smiled, nodding. Then the Spanish-Italian druglord reached for a kilo brick.

And Engels slammed down the lid with all his strength.

A sickening crack of bone.

Salviche screamed.

"But not from me, you greasy-face half-breed," Engels snarled.

The druglord's muscle reacted, but assault rifles swung their way. They froze.

Salviche dropped to one knee, his face a twisted mask of agony. He turned around, wondered why his men didn't do something. Then he remembered why. His men had been stripped of weapons as soon as they'd stepped off the planes.

"What the hell is this, man?" Salviche cried.

His men appeared to him like helpless infants, like mannequins. He wanted to curse them. A seething hatred filled him.

Engels bunched up a handful of Salviche's hair, wrenched the druglord's head back.

If Salviche had thought before that Engels was crazy, now he definitely knew the bastard was insane. The renegade op's eyes looked as if they belonged to some rabid animal. Or to a demon straight from hell.

Certainly they didn't look as if they belonged to anything human.

"Hey," Engels spit. "I'll tell you and your pretty boys here what this is all about."

He pressed down on the lid.

Salviche grimaced. A tear broke from his eye.

"Look at you," Engels snarled, spittle flying from his mouth, spraying Salviche's face. "You're still the same, sniveling, chickenshit punk grease-face I found in that sleazy, slut-stinking hole. Remember? Where you were wiping down toilets and picking up the garbage and whining to me about how you had to make the big time. Yeah, how quickly you punks forget your humble origins."

"Hey, all I ask for is a bigger piece of the action."

"Shut your face!" Engels snarled, his voice hoarse, choked by rage. "You'll be lucky if you walk out of here alive, punk. And you won't ever see your New York again, and your cocaine parties, and your sluts, and your fancy cars and clothes and diamonds, if I don't see a change in your spick attitude. And quick. Don't ever assume you deserve a bigger cut. Don't ever think you're something special around me. You started out with nothing because that's what you were. Nothing. Zero. *Nada*. And you're still nothing. And if you ever think you're a big enough man to strike out on your own, or if you and your spaghetti-suckin' dago buddy think you can hook up with the Mob, you'll both be dead nothings. Just like your garbage-can friends, Maraquez and Diablo.

"Who do you think keeps you in all that coke? You don't think those uptown sluts come running because of your charm and good looks, do you?"

Engels's face turned beet-red from his blind fury. As he straightened and pulled his hand away from the lid of the crate, Salviche thudded to the floor on his side.

A cold silence filled the room.

Clutching his ravaged hand, Salviche trembled violently. He knew his fingers were broken. The pain seemed to shoot all the way up through his arm and shoulder, pierce straight into his throbbing brain. The room, faces appeared to swim around above him in foggy circles.

"Go back and sit in your nice little toys," Engels snarled. "I wouldn't want either of you or your flunkies to get your Gucci suits soiled. When the others arrive, then I'll deal with you, and not until then. Now get up." He lashed out with a kick into Salviche's backside.

Salviche crawled away from Engels until he felt he was out of striking range and could stand.

"This is madness, Engels," Bozzarelli said. "We have done you right. How can you treat us like this? We..."

"You haven't done anybody right but yourselves!" Engels raged on, jabbing a finger toward the thickset Italian. "You're so proud and stupid you can't even see when you've been used. If all of you die out here in this hellhole it'll be a fitting end to your stinking, no-account lives. I was the one who pulled you out of that sewer you call a city. And if I want to, I'll feed you to these snakes. Because I've got the power here. I own this desert.''

Salviche and Bozzarelli looked at each other.

"Don't try taking off, either," Engles warned. "I'll blow you right out of the sky. Now, get the hell out of here. But before you go, chew on this while you're sitting in your planes, brooding and whining. I'm doubling the price this time. Cut, too. And I hope for your sakes you can come up with the price I'm asking. You'll know that price when the time comes. And if you can't cough it up, you'll be coughing up your guts.''

One last glimmer of defiant hatred cut through the pain in Salviche's eyes. Somehow, the druglord swore to himself, he would make Engels pay for this treachery and humiliation. Somehow.

Salviche looked at his own men. The way they avoided eye contact with him, he had the feeling they were laughing at him in their silence.

"I don't like that look in your eyes, amigo." Engels's voice sounded ominous. "I can almost see your mind working. You're thinking about how you can get even for this. Right?''

Engels smiled his cold smile.

Salviche couldn't remember ever hating a man more than he did Engels at that moment. "No," the druglord lied and hoped he sounded convincing. "I just want to carry through with our deal. So that I can leave this hole.''

"Yeah," Engels said. "You'll be leaving this hole all right. Amigo.''

Katterhagen opened the door.

Salviche turned, felt the harsh sunlight stab into his eyes.

"Let us leave this place, Armando," Bozzarelli urged, then muttered something to himself in Italian.

When the druglords and their muscle had filed out of the room, Katterhagen slammed the door shut. The big German and the other Apocalypse Brigade soldiers chuckled.

Engels was the only one in the room who didn't laugh. He turned toward the cages filled with snakes, and stared at the serpents as if mesmerized.

IT WAS SUPPOSED to have been a recon, a thorough surveillance of the hardsite perimeter so Bolan could determine the enemy numbers and plan the course of action for his killing penetration.

But a figure seemed to appear out of nowhere, as if he'd sensed the lone stalker that was the Executioner scaling up the rough-cut south side of the high hill.

The Executioner snaked out the silenced Beretta 93-R from the speed rig beneath his left arm. The Beretta coughed discreetly, sending a 9 mm slug through the soldier's eye, turning his look of surprise into a death mask of agony and shock. The man crumpled, plunged down the hill. Lifeless arms and legs flopped past Bolan, who climbed the remaining six yards to the top of the hill in seconds.

The land behind Bolan was a stark vista of barren, jagged hills and peaks. The desert floor rolled to the south like a rippled brown blanket. The violence of nature had long since sliced this scorched earth with canyons and arroyos. Bolan had hidden his Jimmy in a cave deep in a gorge, front end pointing out in case he had to make a hasty getaway, a long run back across open desert and a fast exit from that canyon.

Bolan had sighted the highest hill from the canyon and chosen it as his point of surveillance. He now knew soldiers were patrolling these hills.

But he'd been spotted. Or was it just pure chance that the soldier walked to the area Bolan had climbed? Whichever, the Executioner was ready to strike. The .44 AutoMag rode in quickdraw leather on his hip. Little Lightning was strapped across his shoulder. Canvas pouches worn across his waist carried extra ammo clips for all three pieces of hardware, and the binoculars were packed in leather, hugging his hip. A wire garrote and a sheathed combat knife completed his gear.

There was no point in taking chances. Not even a seasoned warrior who had survived countless battles like Mack Bolan could always call the shots.

The Executioner could now see he had gotten a complete and accurate description of the land from Young Eagle back at the village. The young Indian, disappointed as he'd been at not being allowed to tag along with Bolan on his warhunt, had scratched the layout of the land in the dirt. The Navaho brave had drawn in every canyon, hill and peak, complete with almost down-to-the-yard distances that separated the land features. Bolan was impressed by Young Eagle's memory, and he made a mental note to tell Young

Eagle that if he ever needed a recon man then the Navaho was it, no questions asked.

Crouching, Bolan slid down along the top of the hill. Silently, swiftly, he moved from boulder to boulder, keeping himself hidden from the eyes of any roving guard. The sun beat down on his neck. He could feel the trickles of sweat running down his body.

About two hundred yards to the north Bolan saw the compound. He counted a group of ten men, dressed like civilians, walking away from a wooden hut toward two turboprop Cheyennes. Rocks and boulders littered the desert floor that stretched west, away from the mountain foothills. A crude airstrip had been secured, cleared free of rock and brush. Unlit flares flanked both sides of the makeshift runway.

Ready for a night landing, Bolan thought. Tonight maybe. It would take a very skilled or very crazy pilot to set wheels down at night on that stretch of cleared desert.

With his field glasses, Bolan looked more closely at the group of men. The sun was behind him, so he knew there was no chance of sunlight reflecting off the lens and alerting someone to his position.

Bolan noted the taut, angry expressions on the faces of the men moving toward the planes. Those guys definitely weren't civilians, either, the Executioner knew. At least not the taxpaying, law-abiding kind. Bolan checked out their expensive threads, saw the sunlight glinting off the gold and diamonds around their necks and fingers.

They couldn't be anything other than the drug-dealing scum Kiley had mentioned, Bolan knew. They sure had that seedy, oily look, the look of a maggot searching for a fresh piece of garbage to suck on. A look he'd seen more times than he cared to remember.

Bolan scanned the foothills. Situated behind rocks, up and down the foothills, were a half dozen soldiers, each armed with an assault rifle.

Bolan counted another dozen brown-uniformed soldiers walking in front of the thirty-yard stretch of wooden quarters along the southwest bend of the foothills. He watched intently as the they hustled along a group of crate-carrying Navaho and Mexicans.

The group disappeared into what looked like a narrow ravine to Bolan, but he couldn't be sure because they vanished behind an outcrop of rock.

Bolan then noticed something very large and bulky beneath a brown camouflage net at the far north end of the runway.

A cargo plane. Couldn't be anything else, Bolan told himself.

Then, about fifty yards off to the side of the runway, toward the foothills, he discovered the large snout of a howitzer jutting up from behind another rocky outcrop.

All of this was military equipment. The cargo plane must have been hijacked, the howitzer stolen, he decided. A man like Engels, with his contacts and connections, certainly had ways of getting his hands on big transport aircraft and heavy firepower if he wanted to badly enough.

The Executioner planned his attack. Tonight he would come in from the east on foot. Dressed in combat blacksuit, he'd make his way along the base of the foothills. He glanced up at the sky. Not a cloud. Good. And there'd be a full moon tonight. If someone was flying in then those flares would be lit, giving some extra light to guide him across the rugged terrain. Night vision goggles would help, too. And the soldier he'd just iced proved to be an asset.

Bolan looked back down the hill at the dead man, judged him to be roughly the same size as himself. After penetrating the outer defenses, the Executioner would don the soldier's brown garb. He needed all the edge he could find to get him inside the compound.

From there, Bolan would take out one man at a time.

"Hey, Toby."

Bolan froze.

"What are you doing up there, man, sleeping?"

So, it had been pure chance. Only the dead man had known Bolan made his way up the hill.

The Executioner listened to boots crunching over loose soil nearby, and closing in.

"Hey, Toby! Where the hell are you? Answer me."

"Taking a dump back here, man. You mind?" Bolan muffled his voice behind boulder.

The soldier appeared suddenly along the hill's edge, just yards away from Bolan.

"Hey, you're not—"

"You got that right, guy."

An HK-91 swung toward Bolan.

The Beretta spoke first, chugged a parabellum slug that drilled through the soldier's forehead and dropped him where he stood.

Bolan was up and running as the corpse toppled, draping itself over a rock. The Executioner hauled the body from the rock, hoping no one had seen the kill.

The radio on the dead man's gun belt crackled to life.

"Herbie. Come in. What are you and Toby doing up there? No, don't tell me. I can guess."

Bolan listened to the laughter on the other end.

"I know you guys are a little funny. Some of the boys are starting to get a little worried about you two."

Bolan picked up the radio. He tried to make his voice sound gruff and hostile, like the dead Herbie's, as he growled, "Yeah, yeah. You guys are real funny. I was keeping an eye on the south side, in case you're interested. Got my eyes peeled until those chopper teams get back with some kind of word. By the way, what's the story on that situation? Over."

"The story is the colonel's going apeshit. Can't raise any radio contact with those choppers. Over."

"Then something's gone down? Over."

"If it has, then the shit's about to fly, buddy boy. Engels just laid it down real hard on that punk, Salviche. Yeah, I'd say the situation's getting tense and ugly real quick. If something's happened to those chopper teams Engels says he'll give free rein to Katterhagen. And you know what that means. Over."

Bolan risked blowing his cover with what he asked next, but he had to chance it. "No, I don't. All this waiting in the sun must be doing something to my head. Spill it out. Over."

"Well, hardhead, it means everybody within a fifty-mile radius of here gets wasted. That's terminate with extreme prejudice. We make that trade-off and get the hell out of here by dawn. It's bye-bye, and overseas time. Palestine's waiting for us with open arms. That's the word from the big man. Over."

Bolan knew he wasn't running out of time anymore.

He *was* out of time.

"What about those Indians?" he asked. "Over."

"Indians? Hell, they're the first to go. And you shouldn't be sweating over this stuff anyway. Over."

"Okay, okay, so I wanted to jaw a little. I'll be in touch. I'll be watching the south side. Over."

"Hey, keep me posted. By the hour. I don't want to have to go searching all over hell's creation for you two anymore. Over."

"Roger that. Over. And out."

One hour, Bolan thought. Then when he didn't check in they'd come looking.

Hard decision time.

Battle time.

Bolan opted to haul ass, double-time it back to the village. Heart Sun and the Navaho were in immediate danger. If they didn't leave, and quick, Bolan knew they'd be slaughtered.

Engels was going to lay waste anything and everything that moved.

Scorched-earth policy.

Then Engels would check out, clean as a whistle.

Well, Bolan decided, it just wasn't going to work out like that.

It was going to be a long night.

One long, hot night in hell.

At that moment, he wasn't certain whether he was going to take the fight to Engels, or if the savages were going to bring the fight to him, particularly since Bolan had to backtrack to the village, round up the Navaho and get them on their way across the desert.

It didn't matter anymore who brought the fight to whom.

The Executioner was combat hard and ready.

He was going to do some wasting and terminating with extreme prejudice of his own.

Mack the bastard Bolan had his own scorched-earth policy.

And his heart carried all the hellfire he would need to burn the life right out of the renegade scum.

11

Heart Sun felt as if a great weight had been lifted off his shoulders.

The warrior of his vision had come.

Those who died at the hands of the evil *beliganos* would be avenged.

The forces were gathering, he knew, being pulled toward the final conflict. The forces always clashed, he thought.

A man's life, the Navaho chief reflected, was a constant struggle with those forces.

And what about all that man achieved with his hands?

A man can shine like the sun, but then comes the night, the oncoming darkness that is his death.

And at that moment Heart Sun was feeling the approach of his own death. It was something he couldn't explain, rather it was a force he sensed, all around him.

He felt no fear. He had no regrets. What had happened during his life, what he'd seen and known, was meant to be. There was a reason for all the grief and suffering he'd known. And he would soon understand it all.

"A shadow lengthens over me," he murmured to himself in Navaho.

Death.

As a young brave, he recalled, he'd survived many confrontations with death. He had seen its shadow in the eyes of every Apache whom he'd killed, the butchers responsible for the rape, torture and scalping of his wife and mother. He remembered his vengeance hunt, driven by some power that could not be controlled until the wild Apache dogs had been slain.

Even now, he was sitting atop the hill that he'd climbed so many years ago. Even now, he was staring down into the arroyo where he'd slain several of them.

Driven by raw hatred.

And hatred, he knew, was a terrible thing, very much like death. How he had seen, how he had felt—these two forces feeding off each other.

It all came back, so clear, so alive, haunting him.

A great sorrow settled over Heart Sun.

He folded his hands, touched the bridge of his nose with his steepled fingertips. As he closed his eyes, he heard approaching footsteps. Two men. He felt their presence, and he knew who they were without looking.

"Take me," he said in Navaho, "but not the one who comes in the name of life. He will eat you. He will devour your numbers. Your evil will not go unpunished."

Heart Sun opened his eyes, lifted his head and looked up.

Bolan and Young Eagle stood side by side, watching him.

They had been there for several moments, Heart Sun knew, but only Young Eagle understood the meaning of the Death Chant.

"We must go," Heart Sun said, his tone solemn. "They will come and kill us if we remain. But this night, Bolan, belongs to you."

Heart Sun stood.

"And it belongs to death," he finished.

The ancient chief and the Executioner looked at each other.

Heart Sun knew the silence spoke to them both.

THE NAVAHO, SILENT AND SOMBER, gathered around their chief.

The stench of death hung in the air.

Flies buzzed around the scattered carcasses.

Buzzards flocked in the sky above the village.

Bolan heard several of the men grumble their protest about having to leave the village at his insistence.

Heart Sun told the group that they must leave for their own safety, that Bolan had discovered the soldiers were coming to massacre them. Heart Sun told the men to forget their foolish pride.

Still, some of them continued to protest, saying it was cowardice to abandon the village and flee into the desert.

"And what would you have us do, John Wind Song?" Heart Sun asked. "Do we have guns to fight these men when they come here? And what about your women? And your children? Shall we let them be slaughtered because of your pride?"

The men stiffened, shifting their gazes away from their leader.

The hottest part of the day was just about over, Bolan figured, and there were still two, maybe three hours of daylight left to guide the villagers on their way across the desert.

Bolan wished he could accompany these people to wherever it was Heart Sun intended to take them. But the best way to defend them, he knew, was to attack and wipe out Engels and his bunch.

"We go then," Heart Sun announced to his people.

With their few meager possessions, rabbit-hide pouches filled with water and sacks stuffed with corn, the Navaho set out across the desert.

Heart Sun and Young Eagle lingered, looking at Bolan.

"Good luck, Bolan," Heart Sun said. "I have prayed that we will meet again soon. I am proud to know you. There were many days when I believed there were no warriors left. But you have made my heart glad to see that I was wrong."

Despite his words, there was a fatal tonality in Heart Sun's voice. Bolan suddenly found himself thinking back on many of the things the chief had told him in just such a voice.

The visions of doom.

The great clouds of fire.

The sea of ashes.

The death of the Indian culture as Heart Sun once knew it.

The dawn of a new world, one that the ancient Indian, Heart Sun, understood and realized he had to accept even if he really didn't want to.

Finally, Bolan recalled what Heart Sun had said about the inevitable fall of every race, every culture of man that had risen to prominence through conquest and invasion.

Just what was ahead, Bolan wondered.

When would his War Everlasting end?

Never, he knew.

Only in his death would it end.

And, then, he had to ask himself, who would carry on the good fight to protect all that was sacred in life? Who would stand up and risk his life, time and again, to preserve the sanctity of life?

Someone would, Bolan hoped. But, perhaps, he feared, no one would. In an age where madness threatened to reign, where greed dominated much of the free world, there were just too few good men.

And too damn many cannibals.

"Take care until I get back, Heart Sun. Young Eagle," Bolan said, "I'd better be going."

Heart Sun nodded. "Yes," he said, placing a hand on Young Eagle's shoulder.

Slowly, they turned away from Bolan, began walking after the departing Navaho.

The sun hung still for a moment, a flaming red smear to the west.

The Executioner looked up at the late-afternoon sky, the stench of death cloying in his nostrils. For some reason he found himself cursing the swarm of vultures overhead. They were searching for the dead, feeding off death. Like animal man.

For another moment Bolan watched the Navaho trudging away from the village, wondered if he would ever see Heart Sun again.

For he had seen something in the chief's eyes, something that made him afraid for Heart Sun and the others. He wasn't certain what it was he'd seen, but it had been something haunting, shadowy in Heart Sun's gaze. Something only a man who had seen death many times could see.

But Bolan had no time to think about it.

War called the Executioner, and he moved toward his Jimmy quickly.

Right then Mack Bolan could only pray for the safety of Heart Sun and his people.

Right then, yeah.

Hell night was about to begin.

And the Executioner had a rendezvous to keep with some demons that needed torching.

12

Armando Salviche was in a state of murderous fury, not to mention agonizing pain. He looked at his misshapen hand, the black-and-blue stumps that were his fingers. The steady throbbing in his injured hand seemed to pulse all the way up through his arm, stopping only at some point behind his eyes.

Bozzarelli sat next to Salviche on the plane.

Silent, just like the other so-called gunmen he'd recruited, Salviche thought. Why did they all just sit there in cold silence, their expressions dark with brooding, the druglord wondered. Because they were all just worried about their own miserable lives.

The silence fed Salviche's boiling rage. He wondered if they all were laughing at him, mocking him in their silence. And just what the hell good were they to him, anyway, he bitterly asked himself. They were no match for Engels and his renegade cutthroats, men who knew hundreds of ways to kill and maim. With intense hatred, Salviche knew that the only animals these gunmen had ever dealt with had been street punks and burned-out junkies, mere ferrets compared to the great white sharks—Engels and his men.

Salviche's hatred grew even more intense as he recalled how he'd been dropped to his knees by Engels, forced to grovel at the man's feet like some whelp being beaten by its master. That was how Salviche saw it, anyway, and he was certain that was how the others saw it, too.

Murdering Engels would be the only way he would win back any respect. If his own men even had any left. If they ever had any respect for him to begin with.

Sure, Salviche had to admit, Engels was the man responsible for pulling him out of the sewer life in the streets of New York's Hell's Kitchen.

All those years he'd hustled scag for the CIA hotshot. All the money he'd made for himself, and for Engels. Wasted. All the contacts. The women, the clothes, the Cadillacs. And now to discover that Engels had only been using him all along, creating Salviche's dream only to turn it into a nightmare.

Shot to hell.

Shot to shit.

Engels had used the scag as a means to some end.

But to what, Salviche wondered. What did the CIA traitor really want?

Whatever it was, Salviche vowed to himself that the man wouldn't live long enough to see it.

Staring out through the window of his private plane, Salviche decided to confront and kill Engels within the next few hours.

He had to.

Every man in his entourage on that plane must now be as aware of their impending doom as he was, Salviche knew. Engels had gathered together in one spot the last few men who could incriminate him.

He had one goal in mind for Salviche and Bozzarelli, two men who had faithfully peddled his junk—terminate with extreme prejudice. That, Salviche knew, was what these CIA guys called a hit. Perhaps he'd gotten in way over his head. Perhaps he should have stayed in the streets, hustling, scratching and clawing, where he belonged. At least there he was among his own kind. At least there he would have stood a better chance of surviving.

Salviche had gotten a bad feeling about Engels when he first learned about the snuffing of Maraquez and Diablo. But at that time Salviche had hoped the two pigs had gotten tangled up in the fast and brutal underworld of Miami coke peddling, that they had met their end by some Mafia gun instead of Engels's black-hearted assassins.

But now Engels had just dashed that stupid idea, Salviche thought bitterly.

"Armando." Bozzarelli cleared his throat. "What are you thinking?"

Salviche felt a sudden and inexplicable hatred toward his longtime street friend, but at the moment he hated everything and everyone in the world. In less than twenty-four hours, he thought, he had fallen from being king of a mountain of gold and had plunged as a maggot into a valley of shit.

"I am thinking that this would be a very terrible place to have to die," Salviche said, trembling as he fought to control his rage. "I am thinking how some

men's hearts are like this desert. Barren and lifeless."
Salviche's eyes blazed. "Engels has been using us all
along, Damien. He made us from nothing when no
one else in the streets would give us a chance, not even
our own. He let us believe we were something when he
considered us lower than *mierda*."

"Listen, Armando, why don't we just fly out of
here?"

When Salviche turned and looked Bozzarelli dead
in the eyes he thought for a second that he was looking right into a mirror. Salviche saw a man every bit as
frightened and desperate as himself. Loathing stirred
like bile in Salviche's belly.

"Have you looked out that window over there?" he
asked, pointing across the cabin.

Sighing, Bozzarelli turned away from Salviche, a
look of defeat on his face.

"These crazy men brought that cannon all the way
here from Jordan or Pakistan, or wherever," Salviche went on. "Like pirates. And it is there to be used
in just such a situation as this. Engels is a demon. He
doesn't care about anyone's life. Maybe not even his
own. Which makes him very crazy. And very dangerous."

"So what are we going to do, huh?"

"What do we do? I'll tell you what we do." Salviche reached under his seat, pulled out a .357 Colt
Python Magnum. The large revolver shook in his hand
as he showed it to Bozzarelli.

"Don't be crazy," Bozzarelli warned.

"What do you mean, 'don't be crazy'?" Salviche rasped. "You have a better way, fool? They're going to kill us. Watch out," he snapped, rose and bumped his way past Bozzarelli, out into the aisle.

"Listen to me," Salviche said, waving the gun above his head, his damaged hand hanging low by his side as he strode to the front of the cabin.

He turned, searched the nine faces that stared at him. He read the hard eyes, the grim expressions. False bravado, he thought. Inside, they were all quaking with fear. It was something he could sense. It was something he could smell.

"We're not going to sit here like lambs for the slaughter. Sure, we'll go along and play it their way. Engels will have to make a good show for his Palestinian amigos. Then, once they're gone..."

A SMILE SLID ACROSS THE LIPS of Engels. He turned up the volume on the receiver.

"These *cabrones* intend to kill us. All of us. They think they'll just leave us behind in this desert to rot for the buzzards. Well, I don't intend to let that happen. I will turn this gun on Engels when he least expects it. You will jump them, take their weapons. But you will kill them only when I tell you. I want that understood now. They will all die very slowly, and in great pain. Engels will suffer the most.

"They consider us nothing but street punks from the slums of New York. We'll show them how wrong they are. We'll return to our city and word will spread about how we personally terminated this country's 'finest' CIA operatives.''

Engels heard Salviche laugh.

''When does this happen?'' Engels heard someone ask, a voice he didn't recognize. ''And how do we do this?''

''When the time comes. We'll wait, like nothing has happened, until Engels sends for us. I'll strike when we are near the heroin. You will have to act instantly. Leap on his men. Your lives will depend on how quickly you act.''

Engels turned off the receiver. ''Good work, Katterhagen. You did well slipping that bug into their plane.''

Katterhagen, hands clasped behind his back, squared his shoulders. ''But apparently we overlooked some weapons in our search. Salviche must have a gun. Should I search the plane again?''

''No. Let them plot their revenge,'' Engels said. ''It means nothing to me. They mean nothing to me, except as a loose end that needs to be tied up. It will all be over soon. We make the trade with the PLO. We then fly behind Azalbha to Jordan. With the cash we'll have in hand I can supply Middle East terrorists with anything they'll need. And with what I know about Company operations in the Middle East . . .''

Engels's smile widened as he walked toward one of the glass cages filled with snakes. There, he stood, staring down at the mass of entwined, scaly flesh.

''We'll be gods over there, Katterhagen,'' Engels said. ''Within five years we'll be financing and controlling every major terrorist group and activity in the Middle East. We plan, organize ourselves and launch an all-out massive strike with combined PLO forces against the West. We will see Israel surrounded and crumbling, finally, to ashes and dust.

"We'll be the Four Horsemen of the Apocalypse. The whole world will know and fear our names. We will rule by death and destruction. We will have the power to save and spare lives. There are great plans to be made. The whole world, Katterhagen! Think, man, think! The whole world is ours for the taking. We have a fortune right here. Millions of dollars' worth of drugs and guns. We have power!"

Engels threw out a clenched fist toward Katterhagen, the hand shaking as if Engels crushed an imaginary globe to fine powder in that fist.

Katterhagen nodded his approval, his eyes like dark pinpoints behind hooded lids. "Yes, yes. It will all happen again, as you say. It is our destiny. We will rule. We *will* rule!"

The shades had been pulled down and only several shafts of fractured light spilled into the room. That was the way Engels liked it, dark, gloomy. Sunlight always hurt his eyes after several hours of exposure.

It was the night that Engels preferred. The night was for stalking and killing. He'd always done his best work at night.

As he gazed at the fat, unmoving bodies of his serpents, he thought back to the times when he'd terminated targets with snakes.

The bushmaster in El Salvador he'd used on a black market arms dealer who'd developed a sense of self-importance that Engels hadn't cared for.

The king cobra he'd bagged in India, then used in Thailand to take care of a certain greedy warlord who'd refused to let Engels in on the heroin trafficking that went out of Southeast Asia.

The snake, Engels thought, so deadly, so beautiful.

"Have you ever stopped and thought, Katterhagen," he said quietly, "that throughout history the snake has been a creature both feared and revered by all men. From shepherd to Pharaoh. It inspires terror, or revulsion, or reverence in all men. If I could, I'd fill every inch of this land with them before we leave. As testimony that we have been here. Men, like the snake, who should be feared and held in awe," he said, his voice trailing off into a whisper.

The door opened.

Engels wheeled, blinded for several seconds by the sudden flood of sunlight.

"Shut the door!" Engels rasped, squinting, stepping toward the big, heavily muscled man with the scar on his cheek.

"What is it, Compton?" Engels growled as the door was shut, the two men facing each other then in the shadows.

"Sir, someone's penetrated our perimeter. Reporting that Thompson and Saunders are dead. Shot at close range, in the face. The weapon had a silencer, must have, or we would have heard the shots."

Engels felt himself freeze. Since that morning he hadn't given whatever enemy might be out there on the desert a second thought. He could see now that he should have. He could see now that he should have done more than just double the guard. Hell, he told himself, but they are all jungle fighters, their ears trained to detect the slightest noise, their eyes like a hawk's, able to catch any movement, spot the least telltale sign of dust in the distance that would betray the position of an approaching enemy.

Now, two more were dead.

Engels wondered how this could be happening.

Only a ghost could move across that desert and cut through their defenses without being seen.

There was only one man Engels knew of who could move like that. One man he had heard plenty about over the past several years.

Mack Bolan.

The Executioner.

Engels couldn't even remember what the man looked like, it was such a long time since his days in Vietnam. But for some reason a tall, shadowy figure was looming large in his mind.

"Where were they found?" Engels asked.

"Just south of here, sir. Over the hills. We followed one set of tracks back to the canyon. From there he left by some kind of 4x4 vehicle, heading due south it looked like."

"Toward the Navaho village," Katterhagen injected. "He must be waiting for night before he strikes again. He'll be hiding with the Indians until then, I bet.''

"Yes," Engels allowed. "Exactly what I'm thinking, Katterhagen. Something keeps troubling me about all of this."

"What's that, sir?"

"Something's telling me we're faced with a situation that's set to explode. The sooner we get rid of those punks out in that plane, the sooner Azalbha is here and gone with the shipment, the better. Something, or someone, is closing in on our operation. We couldn't be leaving here a second too soon. Katterhagen, take three jeeps and some men. Ride out, but give yourselves some time between each vehicle, just in case our man's out there, waiting. I want every last one of those Indians killed and that village leveled."

Engels paused heavily.

A strange light showed in Katterhagen's eyes.

"We're leaving tonight," Engels added. "And we take no prisoners. Anyone left behind is snake food."

And Engels knew that something terrible was indeed about to happen. It was just a feeling he couldn't shake himself free from.

Mack Bolan kept growing larger in his mind.

13

Bolan circled the hardsite far to the west, then moved down toward the compound from the north.

His Jimmy covered by brush, Bolan climbed to the top of a hill, and from there, using his high-powered binoculars, he made one last thorough recon of the enemy grounds.

He scoped a group of men out on the runway. They were gathered around a jeep and one other vehicle.

Bolan adjusted the focus, looked closely at the group, searching their faces.

The other vehicle appeared to be some sort of civilian car, and one guy beside it wore a cowboy hat,...

Bolan felt his blood run cold.

Among that pack of cannibals he'd just spotted Colonel John Travers.

Ex-Green Beret.

Commander of the New Mexico Highway Patrol.

Traitor.

Bastard.

Dirt.

Viciously, Bolan swore to himself.

He had a decision to make right then.

With mounting rage, Bolan watched with intensity.

A guy whom Bolan judged to be the leader, and who appeared to fit the description of Engels that he'd gotten from Hal Brognola's intel and pics via The Strongbase computer, handed Travers a large brown envelope.

Bolan felt the fury expand in his guts.

So Travers had been in on the operation from the start. How many other lawmen had been contaminated by Engels and Travers, Bolan wondered.

A man, a father, was taking money from the very animals who had slaughtered his son!

Bolan couldn't let Travers leave the desert alive.

Target: one dirty lawman.

Now the Executioner was beginning to understand how Engels had been able to operate so smooth and free out on this desert. Now he saw why the Indians had been terrorized without the law stepping in and taking action.

Travers had handled all of that from his end. Perhaps a bribe here to someone wise to him on the force, a bribe there to someone in Gila Plains who knew too much.

Yeah, cash in hand.

Dirty money.

See no evil. Hear no evil.

Travers, Bolan guessed, must have known Engels from Nam. Engels must have some dirt on the ex-Special Forces man, or have exploited some weakness in Travers. Money. Sex, maybe.

Whatever it was, Mack Bolan was going to find out.

He thought about Jamie all of a sudden. Bolan's nagging suspicion that her life might be in danger had just been confirmed by what he saw.

Bolan watched as Engels and Travers exchanged words. Travers appeared angry, while Engels seemed to be trying to placate the lawman.

Finally, Travers turned away from Engels, hopped into his unmarked cruiser.

The car traveled south, then Bolan saw it swing east, disappear behind the southern rock outcrop.

Bolan ran back down the hill, toward his Jimmy.

He knew he'd have to hustle to intercept Travers.

Bolan had to know just how far the poison had spread before this night erupted into hellfire.

The Executioner's countdown to a desert holocaust had begun, and the fuse was burning low, dangerously low toward detonation.

One Colonel John Travers would be the first piece of dirt to get swept away by Bolan's cleansing fury.

Blazing guns.

Butt-kicking time.

The brush flew into the air as the 4x4 shot away from the hill.

IT WAS A DAMNED GOOD THING, Travers told himself, that the bastards who'd gunned down his boy were dead, or he would have just started blowing heads off back on that runway.

Then Travers stopped himself and thought clearly about the insanity of such actions. No, he couldn't have done that. Besides, he reasoned, justice already prevailed for his son.

And justice had come in the name of Mack Bolan, or so he'd been told by Engels. But from what Travers knew of Bolan back in Vietnam and had heard about the man over the past few years, he had no reason to doubt that the hellblazer who reaped a bloody harvest of carnage on Engels's men back at Gila Plains was indeed the Executioner.

Someone John Travers didn't particularly care to meet again.

Now more than ever, Travers figured, he needed Engels. Engels and his guns, the lawman hoped, would be the ones who would have to face down Bolan, and that would take the heat off him.

So if it went that way, with Engels falling to Bolan's guns, Travers would be free of the Engels curse once and for all.

John Engels, Travers knew, was a very powerful man in a shadowy mercenary netherworld that Travers had long since been out of touch with. The dirt Engels had on him went all the way back to Nam.

It was as if the spook had been keeping tabs on him over the years, Travers bitterly reflected, biding his time, searching out all those he could use. A curse that began in Vietnam.

There had been those unsanctioned hits in Cambodia and Laos, extracurricular activities, Travers called them then. And what had finally damned Travers had been the innocent Cambodians who'd been cut down in a cross fire between Travers and his squad and some

NVA regulars. If it hadn't been for Engels and some-body very high up in the military hierarchy covering up the whole atrocity, an obvious U.S.-related inter-national incident would have sparked an investiga-tion. And Travers's brilliant, much-decorated Special Forces career would have been smeared by innocent blood. Not to mention a lengthy stay in prison. Not to mention disgrace and court-martial.

The slaughter that raged out of control in that vil-lage in the Cambodian jungle, Travers recalled, would have made My Lai look excusable by comparison.

Only later did Travers learn that Engels was the man who planned that particular operation for Dragon Company of the Sixth SFG. And it was not until long after the war that Travers found out Engels had set up the fateful mission so that two men in Travers's squad—men who were now soldiers under Engels's command—could smuggle opium from an NVA con-tact back across the border for the spook.

Soldiers Brian Compton and Toby Saunders.

Travers remembered them as gung-ho, kill-crazy rebellious types. Two soldiers who always seemed to be the first ones into a firefight, and the last ones out of a killzone. When it came to killing, they had a nose for blood like a buzzard for carrion, Travers thought.

"Give us your hearts and minds or we'll burn down your goddamned village," Compton used to say.

"If you grab them by the balls, the heart and mind will follow," Saunders used to tell the squad.

Finally, to add insult to injury, Travers had learned from Engels that the whole slaughter was the result of some double-cross between the soldiers-gone-bad and the NVA.

That massacre still haunted Travers. Over the past several years the horrible memory had begun to fade as he remembered instead, and openly talked about to his son and to his buddies on the highway patrol, how he'd won several Purple Hearts and a Medal of Honor.

Booze and long weekend runs to Vegas helped shrink the pain of the memories, too. But the drinking got harder, and large gambling debts began to pile up. For a while he kept it all a secret. That was until John Engels showed up one morning on his doorstep with black-and-white pics of the massacred Cambodians Travers had so desperately tried to forget.

No, Engels had not come there to blackmail him. Quite the contrary. Engels had only wanted to help him, offer him a way to save his lawman career and pay off his gambling debts to certain Vegas creditors.

But there was a price, after all, for the Spook's silence. No one, Travers sarcastically thought, did anything anymore out of the goodness of his heart. Money ran the stinking world. And love? Well, hell, if a man had a fistful of dollars he didn't need a whole lot else. Love could be bought, in twos or threes.

Engels, Travers knew, believed this, too. And Travers could have all the money he wanted if he did everything in his power to keep anyone, civilian or lawman, from snooping around near the compound that Engels wanted built and held down as a secret base for several months. There would be killing, Engels warned, plenty of killing if anyone discovered their operations.

That warning turned out to be a promise.

And lately the Feds had been practically up his ass, Travers thought. How much longer could he keep lying, covering up for Engels and himself? Even firefights in the street of a nothing town out in the middle of nowhere tended to attract attention. And the Feds weren't going to let them alone any time soon. Right now they were in the process of launching a full-scale investigation.

On his way out to collect part of his payment from Engels, he had decided it was over for him.

Not yet, Engels told him.

It seemed the spook wanted him to tie up one more loose end. By that, Engels meant terminating the woman who would've been Travers's daughter-in-law.

Sure, she suspected something, and Travers had sensed it all along. When pressed by Engels about her, Travers had admitted his suspicions, and he now wished he'd kept his mouth shut about it.

She had to die, was all Engels said.

Up yours, get someone else to do it, had been Travers's answer.

That was when Engels decided some blackmail was finally in order.

Now, the future seemed as black as ever.

All right, Travers told himself, he'd go ahead and snuff her. There was something about having to waste a pregnant woman, though, that didn't quite sit right with him. But it was snuff her or spend the rest of his life looking out at the world from behind bars.

And there were a lot of faggots in prison, he knew, a whole lot of them. Somehow the prospect of having to snuff a pregnant woman who might send him to prison suddenly seemed a whole lot brighter. As a lawman he would have it far worse than any punk-turned-inmate. In prison, they really loved the John Wayne types.

Okay, Travers thought. He'd take her for a ride up north. Canyon, mountain country there. Somehow he'd have to kill one of Engels's men, a bloodless snuffing, strangulation, he thought. Then knock the woman unconscious. Put the two of them in his car. Torch the car, and roll it down into a gorge. The bodies would be burned beyond recognition. It would look like an accident, he hoped. But even if an investigation turned up something, he'd be long gone, with enough cash in his pockets to set himself up in South America, maybe the West Indies. Someplace scenic and peaceful. Someplace far, far away from all the madness and desperation.

Travers reasoned that he was a very desperate man, after all. And a damn good man. A man who'd served his country faithfully, far above and beyond the call of duty. A man who'd endured more hell than any one man had a right to endure. He'd paid his dues, some very hard dues.

It wasn't his fault, dammit, that his son didn't listen to him and lay off trying to hunt down the killers of those G-men. It wasn't his fault Kent was dead,

God rest his soul. It wasn't his fault, Travers thought, that he'd come home to a wife he couldn't communicate with, a woman who would have been appalled, would have even hated him for what he'd done over there in a nightmare he hadn't created.

To hell with the whole world, he thought. None of them understood anyway.

Circumstances had simply taken his life beyond his own control. As tough, as gutsy as he knew he was, he was still only one man. And he was no match for fate.

Fate was Mack Bolan, he suddenly thought. And Travers was glad the bastard he'd confronted back in Gila Plains was Engels's problem, and not his.

Travers turned off the main highway, followed a long, winding dirt road that cut through a chain of hills. In the distance beyond the hills he saw Jamie's one-story, ranch-style house. Her old Ford pickup was parked in the front yard. Two horses were grazing near the barn. Beside the barn was a large, rusty pump, unused in years, Travers knew, since the artesian well dried up.

Jamie's aunt had died from cancer several years before, the lawman remembered, and Jamie had inherited the house and the land. A sad, lonely-looking dump, Travers thought. Then he forced away such melancholic feelings, knowing he had to concentrate on the ugly job he didn't want, but had to do.

Killing the engine, Travers flung open the door and stepped out of his cruiser. He wondered why he felt so heavy, why every moment was demanding a conscious effort. He looked at the living room through the window. It was a well-furnished home, and he knew Jamie kept up the place with an intense devotion. He'd had several dinners there with her and his son.

Dusk shadowed the sky.

Coldness filled the lawman.

The ball Travers felt in his guts kept knotting tighter and tighter as he walked up to the front door. There he removed his hat and was about to knock when the door opened.

Travers looked at Jamie. There was a glassy sheen about her eyes, and he could tell she'd been crying.

They stood in awkward silence for what seemed like minutes to Travers.

Finally, he cleared his throat and asked, "Jamie, can I come in for a minute, please?"

She appeared to think about it, then moved aside and motioned for Travers to step inside.

In his mind, Travers cursed Engels with vehemence, blamed the spook for what he was about to make Travers do.

The first thing that caught the colonel's eyes were framed portraits of Jamie and Kent together, the pictures spaced evenly along the oak mantel above the fireplace.

While looking at the faces of two young people who were obviously very happy, very much in love, Travers briefly wondered why he could only feel a cold emptiness toward the whole bloody disaster that had claimed his son's life.

Jamie closed the door, stood near it. "That's the first time I think I've ever heard you use that word."

Travers turned, looked Jamie squarely in the eyes. "What's that?"

"Please. You said, 'please.' Maybe you're feeling guilty about something? Like Kent's death?"

Travers took a step toward her, forced a humble, apologetic expression, made a gesture of helplessness with his hands. "Listen, Jamie, I know you and Kent loved each other very much. You had a good life ahead of you both, I know that. Hell, I'm sorry, believe me. There's nobody sorrier than me that this happened."

"I wonder."

There was a flat note of accusation in her voice, and Travers felt something icy spear through him. "What do you mean by that?"

"I just wonder if you can feel sorry about anything."

"Look, girl, I was his father, dammit! I know you don't particularly care for me, and that's your business. But I never insisted once that Kent join the highway patrol. That was his decision."

Jamie drew a deep breath, her gaze falling off the man.

Travers put his hands on Jamie's shoulders, and she seemed to recoil, but stopped as the lawman continued.

"Jamie, I loved my boy. Like any good father, I wanted the best for him. You can't blame me for his death, can you?"

OUTSIDE, A BLACKSUITED SHADOW crept down the length of the front porch. Mack Bolan strained his ears, the .44 AutoMag in his right hand. He caught the conversation between Travers and Jamie. Pressing himself against the wall beside the front door, he listened to the dirty lawman's lies.

No, Bolan thought, maybe she can't blame you, but I sure as hell can.

Big Thunder was the only piece he'd brought along after parking the Jimmy back down the road; it was all he would need to take care of one savage.

As Bolan eavesdropped, he realized that both of them were just inside the door. Quick and cool, he thought. No sense in bulling his way inside. The element of surprise belonged to him.

Rage seemed to churn Bolan's guts as Travers's deception registered like glass chips slicing through the Executioner's insides.

To Mack Bolan there were few things worse than a good soldier who'd gone bad.

"Listen, Jamie, if I was hard on Kent I had my reasons," Bolan heard. "I wanted him to be something I could be proud of. I was seeing things in him I couldn't take."

"God, how can you talk like this about him now?" Jamie cried. "Is that all you can think about? Your stupid pride? This is sick. I just want you to leave. Now. I want to be alone. Kent doesn't deserve this."

"Listen, girl . . ."

"Leave!"

Bolan had heard enough; he made his play.

The Executioner opened the door, glided inside as if he lived there and found himself standing right behind Jamie.

"You heard the lady, Travers."

A snarl cut the lawman's lips, and Travers reacted instantly, insanely, in a way Bolan couldn't have anticipated, but should've guessed.

Travers dropped down by the woman, grabbed her. Using Jamie as a shield from Bolan's gun, he shoved her violently.

The woman cried out in pain and surprise.

Silently Bolan cursed this reckless move as an innocent life was thrown into a potentially lethal line of fire, but a line of fire Bolan wouldn't, couldn't start. Turning the AutoMag away from Jamie, he caught the woman as she collided with him.

Travers turned on Bolan like some carnivorous beast.

A long roundhouse struck out from behind Jamie's head.

Distracted, concerned for the woman's immediate safety, Bolan took the thunderous blow, felt it smack against his jaw. Stars danced in his vision, and the blow sent him reeling, with the woman, to the floor.

Travers pounced on top of Bolan as the Executioner and Jamie became a tangle of arms and legs.

Bolan lashed out with a left hook, felt bone slam off bone. The crack of Travers's blow still ringing in his ears, Bolan found himself locked in a mortal struggle with Travers for control of the AutoMag.

On her hands and knees, Jamie scrambled away from the mass of rolling, grunting flesh.

His free hand like a claw, Travers went for Bolan's throat.

Bolan wrestled Travers off to the side, smashed the lawman's nose into a blood-spewing pulp with a vicious head butt.

An animallike snarl of rage sounded from Travers's throat, and he held onto Bolan's gun hand.

Bolan felt the sheer brute strength of his enemy, a strength held together through the force of seething hatred and agony that turned the lawman's face as crimson as the blood poured from his nose like water from a broken faucet.

Grappling with each other's hands, drenched in blood, they rolled across the carpet.

Bolan suddenly let go of Travers's right hand, whiplashed an elbow across the demonic-looking face staring up at him.

Still, incredibly, Travers held on to the gun hand.

As he felt Travers coil up like a spring beneath him, lunge up from the torso, Bolan jerked back, away from the head butt. Using the backward momentum, Bolan bolted, Travers clutched in his hands. Instantly both men lost their balance from the lightning move and plunged toward a glass-topped coffee table. They dropped through the glass, shards exploding away from them, metal crumpling beneath them.

Bolan felt countless glass slivers digging like needles into his flesh, but ignored the pain.

He knew that the second either one them gained some position of advantage over the other then the fight would be over. Both were Special Forces trained fighters, and Special Forces men fought only one way—to the death. A millisecond was all it would take to crush a windpipe with a knifing hand blow, drive the other's balls up into his guts with a snap knee kick, pluck out an eye with clawed fingertips like an eagle's talons.

Jamie ran toward the kitchen. There was a .22 Winchester leaning against the wall beside the kitchen doorway.

Hands shot out from around the kitchen doorway, and Jamie found herself in the grasp of a big man with an assault rifle. She froze.

Having wrestled himself into a position of dominance over Travers, Bolan drew his fist back, his gun hand still in the lawman's viselike grip.

Then glass crunched, alerted Bolan to some new danger. In the pandemonium, seized by the frenzy of his life-or-death struggle with Travers, he had been unaware of the brown-uniformed soldier who'd moved up behind him.

As he turned his head, Bolan caught the shapes of several more of Engels's soldiers in the periphery of his vision.

Suddenly, Bolan felt as if his head had been split open by the flat pan of a shovel, as he heard the crack of the rifle butt off his skull echo through his mind.

And Bolan felt himself plummet toward the floor. Jagged glass teeth seemed to lunge upward, toward his face.

14

From atop the valley's highest hill, Heart Sun spotted the telltale cloud of dust, far to the north.

It meant only one thing.

They were coming.

He would have to go down into the valley. There, he would confront the soldiers.

Perhaps they would spare his people, he thought.

Perhaps.

But Heart Sun was not counting on chance, or a change of heart.

His people were gathered at the far south end of the valley. They were frightened; he had made certain they were all inside the great hollow between the hills before he'd set out. They were hidden, and they were safe. For the moment.

Heart Sun looked up at the dusty sky.

The day was over.

The time had come.

He had told his people that, no matter what, they were to remain in the hollow and stay completely silent.

If it meant sacrificing his life so that the others would live, then so be it, he decided.

It was what he had planned all along.

The end was near.

It was good.

The force of light, he believed, was about to purge his homeland free of darkness.

All darkness.

THE VOICES SEEMED TO SWIRL around in his head. Bolan felt his brain throbbing in his ears, his head feeling swollen with a pulsating pressure. He tasted the blood in his mouth and spit out a glass sliver.

Gradually, voices broke through the pain that clouded his mind, and he felt his senses returning him to a state of hurting awareness.

From head to foot, Bolan felt as if he'd been worked over by a tire iron.

The Executioner listened to the men around him arguing about what to do with Jamie and him. Rather, he quickly ascertained, they were not so much arguing that they were going to die—that much he knew for sure—but rather what method of killing should be used.

The cannibals sounded as if they were bickering about the finer points of some chess game instead of plotting murder.

"No way. That's too quick and easy for our hero boy there. We'll take him out to the desert where he blew our choppers out of the sky. It kind of looked to me like Sunther and them were getting set to send hero boy for a dive into that snake pit. I think justice would be served for our dead buddies if we finished that job.''

''Don't you think we should take him back to Engels first?''

''Naw. Us taking out this bastard ourselves is going to look real good to Engels. Especially after the others failed.''

Bolan felt hands dig into his shoulders, flipped him onto his back. He found himself staring up through a fog at the snout of an HK-91.

A big, curly-haired man with a scar cutting across the cheek of his simian features stared down at him.

''So, this is Mack Bolan, huh. Sergeant Mercy, they called him in Nam. The Executioner. One-man army. An unbeatable fighting machine. Hey, Travers, how tough's he look now? He bleeds just like the rest of us, and Engels and them were making this dude out to be some sort of killing machine, a walking nuke. Hey, Bolan buddy,'' the man gloated, ''I thought you were supposed to be so tough, man. Yeah, you sure look real tough to me.''

Bolan's vision cleared then, and he focused on each of the five faces hovering around him.

The blows he'd dealt Travers showed, stark and ugly, on the man's face. The lawman's nose was a mashed-in purple lump. There were black circles beneath both eyes and the soft flesh beside his nose was swollen. Blood bubbled out from thin slashes that were his nostrils, trickled down over his lips and onto red-stained teeth now bared in a grimace of pain.

Travers held Jamie, one hand wrapped around her arm, the other holding a revolver pressed against her side.

"Let me thank you, too, Bolan, for returning that rocket launcher you borrowed," Ape Face said. "Tell me something, Bolan, did you really think you were gonna come here and start playing hero against Engels and all of us, huh?"

Bolan said nothing. He'd already bought some time because of this man's perverse desire to see him die in the viper pit. Neither was there any point in riling Ape Face now, or the cannibal just might lose his cool altogether and spread Bolan's brains all over the floor.

"Bet you thought you were gonna save those Indians?" Ape Face taunted. "Is that your special crusade for the week, huh? 'Save the Indian.' Well, suck on this one, boy. Some of us are at the village right now, and they'll be bringing in a whole lot of scalps. I'll be sure to feed you a few when you're down with those snakes, Bolan buddy."

Ape Face laughed.

"Come on, let's get on with it, Compton," Travers growled.

"Shut up, Travers," Compton rasped. "This ain't Nam no more. Engels outranks you here. And don't you forget it again. Or I might forget Engels still has a job for you to do."

"Yeah, all right, well, I'm getting the hell out of here," Travers said.

"Not until you finish that job. Don't forget your girlfriend there."

"Not here," Travers said, his voice low, deadly. "I'm taking her out in the desert."

Compton showed Travers a doubtful look.

"The body, idiot. I don't need the Feds charging out here. They're breathing down my throat now, as it is. I need a couple of days to get free and clear of this mess you and Engels started."

Jamie was speechless with terror, her face pale, her expression taut. "You bas—"

"Shut up!" Travers snarled, squeezing her arm.

"All right, Colonel, but just remember—Engels may check your work later." A crooked smile, then Compton went on. "Only reason I'm letting you go at all is because we go back a long ways. Maybe there was a time when I thought you were a pretty good dude. Maybe I still want to hold on to those sweet memories."

"You're breaking my heart. I should've busted you a long time ago."

"That's the problem with you, Colonel. You're still fighting that war. A dirty war you tried to fight clean. Now, you're a clean dude who's gone dirty."

Travers worked his jawbone, looking at Compton with pure hatred. "Tell Engels I'll be seeing him soon. He still owes me a few bucks. And I intend to collect."

Travers hauled Jamie away, left the house.

"Sure thing, Colonel," Compton muttered.

Bolan raised himself up on his elbows.

There was no sense in damning his misfortune, wasting one moment second-guessing the moves that had gotten him trapped. He'd been taken by complete surprise.

The cards had been dealt.

If there was an ace in the hole, Bolan knew he'd better find it quick.

"Get up, hero boy," Compton said.

Bolan hesitated. No choice but to go along with them. Four guns were trained on him from every direction. Any sudden move now was suicide. And he could see they were all just itching to cut loose with assault rifles.

Bolan thought about Jamie, Heart Sun and the villagers.

As long as he was breathing, he knew there was hope for them.

But that hope was growing dimmer by the second.

Bolan stood.

The muzzle of an HK-91 prodded the Executioner in the back.

Bolan heard Compton laugh behind him.

"Sergeant Mercy. Hey, Sarge, you bring your snakebite kit by chance?"

Just one chance, asshole, Bolan thought. One opening was all he needed.

Yeah, Mack Bolan would go ahead and bide his time.

Live on borrowed time was all he could do at the moment.

But then, that was all he'd ever done.

THEY CAME, AS HE EXPECTED they would.

Alone, in the middle of the valley floor, equidistant from the chain of hills to the north and those to the south, Heart Sun sat, cross-legged.

There was a look of serenity about the chief's wizened features as he stared straight ahead into the two pairs of headlights.

Slowly the jeeps rode across the bumpy desert floor, trailing dust clouds.

Light stabbed at the lone, unmoving figure.

Several yards short of the Navaho chief the jeeps stopped.

Engines died, but headlights stayed on, a white glow washing over the solitary shape of Heart Sun.

Total silence seemed to stretch throughout the valley.

The final fading light of day showed, dark pink streaks to the west.

Six men stepped out of the jeeps, walked to the front of the vehicles. There they stood, dark shapes bathed by white light, their rifles held low by their sides.

Heart Sun shut his eyes. He let the stillness feed the warmth he felt spreading throughout his whole body.

These men, he knew, could not kill him. Physically, yes. But only a fool believes that he lives in his body forever.

These men—with their mindless violence, their evil ambition—were just such fools, Heart Sun thought. In some ways, he pitied them.

"Okay, old man," Heart Sun heard a voice call from the light.

From the dark light.

"Where are the others?"

Heart Sun freed himself from all feeling, rid himself of the memories of the atrocities he had suffered at the hands of the white and the red man alike. He prayed to the Great Spirit that his people would listen to him. If they remained in the darkness where they now were, and stayed silent, he knew these men would never find them.

"Are you deaf, old man? I asked you a question. Don't make me have to get ugly."

What are these years on earth anyway, Heart Sun thought, but a passage, a very short journey? Where one is granted the privilege to enjoy the beauty of the earth. Where one learns about himself and others, if he is wise.

Life, Heart Sun believed, was indeed a privilege, and for some reason he thought his privilege had been extended far beyond normal years. For reasons he was not aware of. Yet.

"Old man, you got about two seconds before I start kicking the shit out of you. Do you hear me? Where are the others?"

Heart Sun heard, but did not listen to the angry, hate-filled voice; he merely let that voice pass through him like sand through a sieve, a hollow, distant sound in his ears, one that really meant nothing to him.

Nothing to him at all.

The only thing that mattered to him was that the others were kept safe from these men. It was for his people that he was ready to offer up his life.

Katterhagen walked up to Heart Sun, stood over the chief as the others formed a tight semicircle around him.

Heart Sun's eyes stayed shut, and he remained as silent as the oncoming darkness. He was at peace with himself, and his heart was filled with joy.

Heart Sun felt as if he was no longer even there.

"We don't have a lot of time to be pissing off around here," Heart Sun heard one of them grumble to the others.

"There's no telling where they've hidden," another said. "They could be anywhere out here. These hills and canyons are loaded with caves and tunnels."

Anger darkened Katterhagen's expression, but Heart Sun didn't look, didn't care.

"Look at me when I'm talking to you, old man."

Heart Sun heard the words passing through him like wind through a canyon. There was a voice deep inside of him, a voice much stronger, much louder than the voice of his tormentor, and he focused on that voice instead. It was a voice that soothed him, drawing him even deeper inside himself until he felt as if he floated in a void.

Katterhagen stooped, lashed Heart Sun across the cheek with a stinging backhand.

Heart Sun turned his head back to face his attacker, his peaceful expression unchanged by the blow. Blood ran from his split lower lip.

Katterhagen straightened, the disbelief in his eyes turning quickly into rage.

One of the soldiers cracked a sardonic grin. "Looks like you're losing your touch, Kat."

"Let's get on with this," one of the other shadows growled. "If you're going to beat it out of him, then do it. We've got to be heading back. I don't intend to be left behind."

"Just shut your hole! I'm in charge here!" Heart Sun heard the man who'd struck him snarl. A man who had far less control over himself than others, a man who then had control over nothing.

Another backhand blow, then an open-palm slap cracked against Heart Sun's face.

Not even a wince broke the Indian's expression.

Katterhagen became incensed. "Where are they?" he screamed. "Do you want to die, you old fool? You will, if you don't tell me where the others are. Do you hear me?"

A voice of fear, Heart Sun decided, the voice of a man ruled by fear.

There was no fear in Heart Sun.

He felt no pain from the blows.

No anger.

No hatred toward those who meant to kill him.

For he was in control. Those two all-powerful, opposing forces of good and evil that separated spiritual man from animal man no longer clashed inside him. There was only the feeling of utter, calm detachment from the dark and brutal world around him.

In his mind, Heart Sun returned to better days. Days long, long ago when he was young, and there were dreams, and there was much to live for even if the Indians' homeland was being invaded.

"I asked you a question, old man, and I swear you'll answer me . . . or I'll kill you right here."

Katterhagen swung his rifle by the barrel, slamming the stock against Heart Sun's jaw, shattering bone.

Together, Katterhagen and another soldier drove their rifle butts into Heart Sun's head, but neither blow, thrown with all their combined strength and fury, dropped the chief.

Heart Sun felt the terrible blows as nothing more than grazing punches. And they did nothing to disturb the final dream.

Enraged beyond reason, Katterhagen began pummeling Heart Sun's head, the stock splintering as it smashed off jaw, skullbone repeatedly.

Blood streamed down Heart Sun's face.

The others joined Katterhagen in his frenzy.

Lightning blow after blow rained down on Heart Sun's head and face, and the chief finally began to slump under their assault, but appeared to be held up, as if by some unseen force.

And he was.

A boot plunged into Heart Sun's stomach; another kick snapped ribs.

A broken rifle stock glanced off the bloodied, misshapen face.

Heart Sun's body thudded to the hard-packed soil, his arms outstretched.

Sweat slicked Katterhagen's face. His rasping breath sawed at the ominous silence. He stared down at the unmoving, blood-drenched body he'd beaten to a pulp.

Fractured shafts of light slanted downward between their bodies, washed over the horribly battered face.

No one said a word.

A crazed, haunted look showed in every pair of dark eyes that stared down at what had been done.

"Let's get out of here," Katterhagen finally said. "It sure doesn't look like we're going to find them now. Old man," he spit at Heart Sun, "you were stupid. See where your pride got you, Indian."

Wheeling, Katterhagen strode for the jeeps.

The others hesitated, but then followed Katterhagen.

Jeep engines fired to life.

Then silence settled again over the valley as the jeeps vanished into the distance.

A low, moaning wind stirred dust near Heart Sun.

BOW IN HAND, his quiver filled with arrows, Young Eagle sprinted through the twilit gloom. From the mesa far to the south, he had seen them ride off, leave behind a fallen body.

Even before he reached the body, Young Eagle knew it was his beloved chief, Heart Sun.

Fear turned into grief when he saw the swollen, bloody Heart Sun, and he wept bitterly.

For a full minute Young Eagle was racked by choking sobs.

Then he felt a powerful hatred and rage fill him. Forcing back tears, Young Eagle stood, his eyes smoldering with vengeance.

He looked up at the darkening sky.

"I will kill them," he vowed, then was seized by an uncontrollable fit of shaking as he pulled an arrow from his quiver and set it in his bow. "I will kill you all, murderers!" he screamed, and shot his arrow toward the sky. "Murderers!"

Young Eagle spun, ran.

The Navaho's bellow of hate and fury seemed to echo after him.

Heart Sun's eyelids fluttered open. His lips cracked. "Young Eagle . . . No . . . No . . ."

15

They kept ten feet between Bolan and themselves, weapons held low at their hips.

That was smart, the Executioner thought. They were out of his immediate striking range.

Bolan was going to change that.

As they ushered him up the gully, toward the top of the hill, Bolan felt the adrenaline dam up inside himself.

He had been in countless act-or-die situations before, and he was determined to get out of this one to carry on his War Everlasting. Turning on an enemy that had captured and intended to kill him, and freeing himself from its bondage wasn't a question of luck, the warrior knew, but rather a matter of waiting and gutting it out. It was a matter of not panicking, while looking for that one millisecond when the enemy would drop its guard.

So far, Bolan noted, they'd taken every precaution to keep him moving along without their having to get close to him. These men were pros, and they weren't taking their advantage for granted.

One soldier kept his flashlight trained on Bolan from behind, another soldier played his flashlight on their captive's face. His eyelids slitted, Bolan made every effort to keep from looking directly into that blinding glare.

The black, twisted hulks of the two assault choppers that Bolan had blown out of the sky now lay down in the ravine. Beside the wreckage Compton had parked his jeep, and another soldier had parked Bolan's Jimmy. There was a lot of firepower in Bolan's vehicle that impressed Compton, and the renegade operative intended to keep it all.

"If I have to shoot you in the legs, bastard," Compton rasped as Bolan neared the top of the gully, "I will. Then drag your ass to that pit myself. Move it, I said!"

Bolan kept his hands clasped against the back of his head. There had been nothing for the soldiers to tie him up with, and that gave Bolan two deadly weapons—his bare hands.

Stars winked from the inky blackness above the desert. A full moon shone above the mesa, beaming down on the shadowy tableau.

As Bolan reached the top of the hill, wind soughed across the small flat area, which then gave way to a high ridge of saw-toothed rock.

"Just think, Bolan," Compton gloated. "You're on your way out. And my ship's just coming in. Yeah, this time tomorrow all of us will be sitting real pretty someplace in the Middle East. With enough cash for each of us to live like oil sheikhs. Big plans, hero boy, and I'm not about to let you spoil them. Dig?''

"What kind of plans?" Bolan asked, and stopped, listening intently to the crunch of boots over soil behind him that betrayed the position of the other two men.

"Stop stalling," Compton said, then shoved Bolan toward the crevice.

The Executioner took an unaided step closer to the edge. There he stood, turned his head. Two soldiers, their shapes outlined only by moonlight, sidled up behind him. They stopped, with rifles lowered, a dozen feet behind Bolan.

Compton pointed the beam of his flashlight down into the pit.

Dry laughter rang out behind Bolan.

The powerful light seemed to agitate the vipers in the pit. They stirred, sliding over skulls, between rib cages. The sound of dozens of rattle rose up from the bottom of the pit.

"Can we get this over with?" Bolan heard one of the two men behind him ask. "This damned place...I can't stand it."

Compton tossed the flashlight back to the soldier who'd voiced his anxiety, then stepped closer to Bolan. "You going to jump in, Mack baby? Or is Pearson there going to have to give you a little help?"

Compton showed Bolan a wide, ugly smile.

It was obvious to Bolan, as he glanced at the man Compton had mentioned, that Pearson didn't like the idea of having to get any closer to their captive than was necessary.

Compton squeezed off a sudden burst.

Bullets traced a line beside Bolan's feet; the Executioner held his ground but felt the icy tremors of fear shooting through him.

"Pearson," Compton growled.

Pearson hesitated.

"Go on!"

Reluctantly, the man moved toward Bolan. Both the assault rifle and the flashlight trembled in Pearson's hands.

Pearson began to lift a foot.

Compton's smile grew wider, uglier.

Something swished through the air.

Behind him, Bolan heard one of the soldiers cry out in pain.

Compton's head jolted sideways as the man behind him dropped to his knees, clutching at something like a stick that protruded from his chest.

Bolan knew immediately what had happened, and galvanized himself into action.

Pearson's nose was crushed like eggshell behind the Executioner's backhand hammer fist.

Compton, with fear now widening his eyes, whirled toward Bolan, swinging his rifle up to fire. But an arrow drilled through the back of Compton's neck, severing his spinal cord, the razor-sharp metal tip punching out through his throat.

Bolan seized the barrel of Pearson's rifle with both hands, keeping the muzzle beside him in a viselike hold. Spinning, Bolan plunged a foot deep into the man's gut.

Air belched from Pearson's lungs. His face contorted with agony and horror. He let go of the rifle, tumbled over the edge.

Unaware that Compton was dead, Bolan, completing his lightning whirl, unleashed a five-round chatter that stitched the cannibal from navel to throat.

Frozen for a heartbeat with terror over the sudden deaths of his comrades, the last Brigade soldier took an arrow through his eye.

Compton thudded on his back as bone-chilling screams ripped through the night, echoing up from the pit.

Bolan turned just in time to see the soldier reach for the arrow speared into his brain. His jaw was slack, his hand shaking as it reached out for the impaling shaft. Then the soldier crumpled to his knees and toppled face first onto the ground.

The silhouette that was Young Eagle lurched up from the gully. Bow in hand, the Navaho stood there for a full second.

Shrieking continued to reverberate behind Bolan. The man's struggle could be heard as he scuffled around in the pit.

Bolan looked down into the pit. He could make out the black, writhing shapes, coiling, lunging around through the thick dust cloud that floated up toward him.

The Executioner triggered a long mercy burst.

An eerie silence stretched across the mesa.

Bolan flinched, turning at the sound of something being sheared off, a blade scraping bone.

Young Eagle had seized a large hunting knife from one of the dead men. Within seconds, he scalped each of the dead.

Moonlight glinted off the Navaho's eyes. There was a frenzied look on Young Eagle's face as he thrust the bloody tufts toward Bolan.

"They killed him. They beat him to death!" he raged, and hurled the scalps into the pit.

Bolan said nothing, allowing Young Eagle to vent his fury. The Executioner didn't have to ask who had been butchered; he could almost see the murder of Heart Sun in the raw hatred that burned in Young Eagle's eyes.

The Executioner forced back his own white-hot fury.

"Where are the others?" he growled.

"They're safe. Heart Sun hid them in the caves to the south. He went out and met the *beliganos*. Alone. I couldn't stop him; he wouldn't let me. Heart Sun sacrificed his life for us."

Bolan's jaw muscles rippled in anger. Heart Sun had saved the lives of his people, and perhaps, Bolan thought, had bought him some time. He owed Heart Sun now, and heads would roll to meet that tab.

"I had a debt to you in my heart, Bolan," Young Eagle said. "Now there is a debt for Heart Sun's murder. I'm going with you. To take what is owed him. Don't try to stop me. I'll follow you anyway. I won't remain behind and do nothing."

Before Bolan could answer one way or another—and his gut instinct was to turn Young Eagle away—movement out on the desert floor to the northeast caught his attention.

The distance and the darkness didn't allow Bolan to make out the vehicle clearly, but he guessed it was one of Engels's patrol jeeps.

Bolan settled a stony gaze on Young Eagle. "All right," he allowed. "But you do what I tell you to, when I tell you to. Got that?"

"I got it."

Bolan kept his warning stare on Young Eagle for a stretched second. He didn't like the tone of Young Eagle's voice. It told the Executioner that trouble had just begun.

Swiftly, Bolan strode away from the carnage.

To greet that patrol crew.

To begin collecting a long overdue tab from the soulless monsters that inhabited the night.

Hell, Bolan grimly decided, let trouble come.

The sound of vibrating rattles floated across the mesa.

JAMIE COULDN'T BELIEVE that the man next to her, the man who was about to murder her in cold blood, was the father of Kent Travers. Or had there been some part of Kent, some darkness in his heart, that he'd kept hidden from her?

No, she decided, and berated herself for thinking such a thought about the man she would have married, a man she'd loved absolutely, and still did in memory.

The darkness around her was total, and she was glad she couldn't see the face of the man who sat beside her.

Headlights stabbed high and low into the pitch-blackness as the cruiser jounced over the uneven desert floor.

There was nothing out there but the buzzards, Jamie thought, with a cynicism that surprised her. Perhaps she just didn't care anymore, she told herself.

Kent was dead.

No marriage.

No home.

What future was there?

Then she remembered the child she was carrying, and with a sudden grim determination, she realized that her future lived on inside of her.

But as she stared out the window, the fire to live dwindled to ashen coals. At present, there was little chance for any kind of future. There wasn't a living soul within forty miles in any direction. She'd been out there, explored the rugged country, the hills and the mountains many times on weekend hikes with Kent.

Amateur archaeologists, they'd probed the Zuni, Pueblo and Aztec ruins. She recalled their childlike zeal as they'd explored the caves and the catacombs, searching for artifacts. Kent had always dreamed aloud about finding the bones of some prehistoric mammal, like the extinct ground sloth, mastodon, or saber-toothed tiger.

She remembered the names because Kent would use them when he wondered what it might have been like if both of them could have stepped back in time and lived in an era when the earth was alive with strange and fascinating creatures that the human eye had never seen in living flesh.

But, then, he was like that, she recalled. A dreamer. A gentle man who had only wanted a simple life. A man who could live and let live.

"Why did you do it?" she quietly asked John Travers.

"Do what?"

His voice sounded cold, lifeless to her, as if it came from a tomb.

"Choose sides," she replied in a voice that now sounded every bit as emotionless to her as his had.

Softly Travers snorted. "Let me tell you something about life, Jamie. Something I've learned the hard way. You never really choose sides. Those sides choose who they want. The older you get, the more you begin to realize that nothing is really ever planned. It's all chance. Like a crapshoot. Things happen. The years pass you by. What you thought was so damned important at twenty or thirty isn't even worth thinking about by the time you reach my age.

"Hell, girl, you're sitting there, judging me like you think I actually wanted Kent to die," he accused.

Jamie sat in cold silence. She felt drained; the fight had gone. No one was going to help her. No one was going to save her. Physically, she was no match for a trained killer like John Travers. Mentally, she was too fatigued to plot some course of action to escape.

"Like everyone else, I've got some regrets, too, Jamie," Travers went on, sounding as if he wanted to apologize, but had injected enough anger into his voice to keep him from doing so. "If I had known what was going to happen I would've done everything in my power to prevent it."

"Like what?" she said sarcastically.

"For starters, I was set up in Nam by some self-serving pig who got my own men to smuggle heroin back into the States for him. Only I didn't know it then. In case you're interested, you're the first person I've ever told this to, and the only reason I'm telling you this is because maybe it will shed some light on all of this insanity. That you're damning me for."

"Are you going to kill me?" she suddenly asked.

The lawman's nostrils flared, and his jawline rippled as he clenched his teeth. "I don't know yet."

"And what about the baby?"

"What about it?" he rasped.

She looked at him, sensed that he was feeling some guilt. It was the baby, she thought. His conscience, though, did her little good at the moment. Death and violence were a way of life with him. He would just kill her, and perhaps forget about it tomorrow when he woke up.

"Life can't always go your way, Jamie," he said in a reflective voice. "Death comes for all of us, sooner or later. Some of us live too damned long, and some of us don't live long enough. If I let you live now, I'll end up paying for a whole lot of wrong that I've already paid for. Paid for inside.''

Jamie couldn't believe what she was hearing—the man was insane. All he could see was his own life, his own turmoil. He was like a blind man to her, and no one else mattered. She felt rage.

''Life certainly hasn't gone my way, by any means,'' he said. ''I've gotten my ass kicked for more than forty years. Every time something lousy would tear my life apart, though, I kept picking myself up. I kept on fighting.''

''I'm bleeding for you,'' she said softly, but with sarcasm.

''Yeah, well, you've got no idea what it's been like to walk in my shoes. You got no idea about all the hell I lived through over there. A hell none of you kids knows anything about. A hell that cost me my wife, and my self-respect. I came back here, and what did I see? Ingratitude. Worse, the whole stinking country is just looking to take some easy way out. Not just out of the war, but anything that involves a little struggle. Life, yeah, life. It wasn't all that different over there, either. Men, young boys, are dying while I'm watching officers getting medals pinned on them for calling the shots from behind a desk. Another guy over here, a spook, making himself a fortune by dipping his hands into black market heroin and by selling arms to the guys who were shooting back at me.

''Back home the civs and hippies are moaning about something they're too damn chickenshit to go and find out about. Yeah, and there I am, getting my ass shot at and being set up to take the heat off a million-dollar illegal operation that went on right under the noses of the very men I was taking orders from.''

Hatred blazed in his eyes as he turned and searched for the woman's face in the dark. "You know, when a man spends his life trying to do good while everyone else is living a lie and using what good he stands for... Hell, you tell me, girl. Wouldn't it eat away at your guts? Wouldn't you be tempted to stick your hands out and take a little of what everyone else is getting at your expense?''

"I would hope... I would hope that I would do whatever's right.''

"Right for who?'' Travers asked, his voice low, laden with scorn.

Jamie looked away from Travers, chilled by the look in his eyes. "How about right for Kent? For starters.''

A mirthless grin stretched Travers's lips. "It's not always as easy as that. The answers just don't come when you need them most. And most of the time, they don't come at all. You react. That's about it. Sometimes, you don't react the way you should, but you react to save yourself. The minute you stop doing that, you're dead.''

Travers stopped the car.

Jamie looked at the man with renewed fear.

Travers shut the engine down, doused the lights, then reached behind the seat. Bringing the pump shotgun into view, Travers cocked it, the action sliding back and forth like an iron door opening and closing.

Jamie felt an icy shiver go down her back.

Travers opened the door, grabbed a flashlight.

"Get out. This side."

Jamie hesitated. This was it, she thought. She felt the panic build.

Travers shone the light on her face. "C'mon, get out."

She slid across the seat, stepping out into the night.

Travers turned off the flashlight, tossed it back onto the seat. The shotgun came up in his hands.

The night, the distant starlit sky seemed to collide, swirl in her eyes. The fear she felt as she waited for the muzzle to erupt in smoke and flames was paralyzing, made her dizzy.

Slowly, Travers lowered the shotgun by his side. "I can't do it. For some reason, I just can't do it.

For a brief moment Jamie experience relief. No matter how dirty the man was, he couldn't shoot a woman in cold blood. It must be the baby.

Travers climbed into his cruiser, shut the door. "I don't have to do it. You're a good forty miles from anyplace," he told her. "No food. And there's no water out here, not even a cactus. Not a bit of shade, unless you want to dig yourself a hole in the ground and wait out the sun tomorrow. But time's something you won't have out here, girl. This time tomorrow, I'll be long gone anyway. I'm sorry it all had to be like this. Really, girl, I am."

Renewed fear numbed her senses again. She wasn't certain she'd heard him correctly at first. She thought she saw regret in his eyes, but in the darkness she couldn't be certain about that, either. His silence made her curious, stretched the fear in her belly taut, like piano wire.

Then it struck her.

He was going to leave her stranded, in the middle of nowhere.

He was going to let the desert kill her.

He was going to let the vultures pick her bones clean.

And, as the engine fired up and he drove away, she realized that it was a very real, and a very frightening possibility.

There was nothing out there.

Except death.

The cruiser's taillights diminished in the distance, flared once, then vanished in the night.

The silence seemed to weigh down on her.

She told herself that no matter what, she was going to survive.

What had that man, Mack Bolan, told her in Gila Plains that morning?

There were reasons for everything that happened in life, even for the worst of troubles, he had said.

Suddenly, she felt grateful to even be alive.

And she had more than just her own life to think of.

The unborn that she carried deserved a chance at life.

BOLAN SAW the jutting, dark shape of a .50-caliber machine gun mounted on a tripod on the back of the jeep. Definitely one of Engels's crew, the Executioner figured.

And they were going to bite the dust.

Wheeling the jeep he'd taken from Compton along the base of the hill, Bolan fisted the mini-Uzi, deciding against manning the .50-caliber behind him. This was going to be a lightning strike, and Bolan wanted to appear as natural as possible. Like he was one of them.

Bolan hit the high beams, headed straight toward the oncoming jeep. Braking the vehicle, he told Young Eagle, "Stay put."

As Bolan stepped out of the jeep, walked near the front of the vehicle and stood beside the harsh glare of headlights, he waved his arm for them to stop.

They did.

Splaying his legs, the Executioner waited.

With his right hand, Bolan slid Big Thunder free of its hip holster.

Lights washed over his face and he opened up with a deafening twin roar of Uzi and AutoMag fire.

One sweep of 9 mm slugs took out the headlights. Bolan hosed the windshield, the light from his own jeep shining on four faces etched in shock and horror.

Glass imploded on those faces, and two heads disintegrated behind waves of razoring glass shards and 9 mm and .44 headbusters.

One guy flung open the passenger door, leaped from the jeep.

Bolan swung his Uzi, stitching the man across the legs, slamming him, screaming, to the ground.

With a desperate lunge, the last soldier with the red armband of the Apocalypse Brigade grabbed the .50-caliber machine gun, but an arrow thunked into the side of his neck an instant before Bolan launched him from the jeep with combined death messages from Little Lightning and Big Thunder.

"I thought I told you something," Bolan growled at Young Eagle, as the Executioner slowly walked up to the cannibal writhing in agony on the ground.

Bolan's boots crunched over glass fragments.

Uzi in his left hand, the AutoMag held low by his side in his right hand, Bolan loomed over the downed enemy.

The Executioner was nothing but a black shape standing in the light from the jeep's headlamps.

"I can make it quick and painless, guy," the Executioner said in a graveyard voice, "or I can leave you to rot. If you're lucky, you'll die before sunup. If not, you'll be unlucky enough to feel the buzzards ripping chunks out of you. And they'll probably start with your eyes."

A hate and pain-filled stare sought out Bolan.

"Where does Engels keep the Navaho? Quick!"

"In the catacombs," the wounded man spit.

"Where are the catacombs?"

"Near the end of the runway," he forced out through gritted teeth, holding his blood-drenched legs.

"There's a ravine.... They'll be dead by the time you get there. You're dead...."

"Thanks," the blacksuited shadow said. "And good night."

Big Thunder roared once.

As Bolan turned, he saw Young Eagle descend on the corpse behind the jeep. Knife in hand, the Navaho fisted a handful of the dead man's hair. The blade arched toward the dead man's forehead.

Bolan's hand clasped over Young Eagle's wrist, the knife shaking violently in the Navaho's fist. Bolan spun Young Eagle around, jerked him to his feet.

"It's one thing to kill a man," Bolan rasped, his gaze icy cold. "It's another to make a sport out of his death. I don't care how much you're hurting by Heart Sun's death, don't let me catch you doing that again. Got me?"

Young Eagle just stared up at Bolan, his dark eyes brimmed with fear.

What Young Eagle had done back on the mesa, and what he'd been prepared to do before being stopped now, brought back memories of Vietnam for Mack Bolan, a war that had brought out the best and the worst in men.

In Nam, Bolan recalled, some grunts who'd scored kills on Charlie had cut the VC's ears off and worn them around their necks or belts like trophies. It had sickened Bolan then to see men making sport out of something as ugly as death.

It had sickened him then, and it sickened him now.

And even though Young Eagle was consumed by a powerful lust for vengeance, Bolan couldn't allow the Navaho to make a mockery out of death.

In death, Bolan believed, there should be dignity— a dignity allowed even for the enemy, for those who didn't deserve that dignity. In a way, even a cannibal's life was sacred, because he had to answer to the same force as anyone else after death. The difference was that the cannibal had wantonly chosen to pervert the sacredness of his life.

And by so doing he endangered the lives of others.

And by so doing he forfeited his right to life.

Bolan turned away from Young Eagle and headed back toward the jeep.

Young Eagle swallowed hard, seemed rooted to the spot by fear.

16

Engels got the thumbs-up sign from his radio man, Hal Davis.

Everything was falling into place, the Company renegade thought. Within the hour everything should be wrapped up, the transactions made, the drug pushers terminated. Then Engels and his cadre of outlaw operatives would be on their way across the Pacific to a new life in a new land.

The Arabs had circled the base in their Bell 222 twin-turbine helicopter on orders from Engels, and were now cleared for a landing. Even though the aircraft belonged to a business contact Engels had established in Jordan many years ago, it never hurt to be cautious. Time, and money, Engels knew, had a funny way of reshaping allegiances.

Engels just wanted to be certain that the Arabs hadn't brought along any unwanted air traffic in the form of backup crews looking to double-cross him, or picked up a roving police helicopter. There'd been plenty of action and surprises that day already, and Engels wasn't in the mood for any more sudden interference from outsiders.

Engels stood off to the side of the runway, his hand draped over the butt of his Colt .45 ACP. A distant look crossed his eyes; he appeared oblivious to the activity around him.

Dozens of flares sizzled and smoked, up and down both sides of the airstrip. Two floodlights on each end of the runway guided the chopper down for the landing.

Katterhagen stood beside Engels. The German, his hands clasped tightly behind his back, looked anxious.

A trio of unmanned jeeps with mounted .50-caliber machine guns were parked just west of the runway. Machine gun muzzles were turned toward the Piper Cheyennes. From behind the windows of each plane, faces showed, outlined by the soft yellow light in the cabins.

Near the wooden quarters, brown-uniformed soldiers with HK-91s and Colt M-16A1 Commandos flanked the group of Navaho and Mexicans carrying crates from the tunnel. Just beyond the mouth of the ravine they piled the crates that the PLO representatives had come to purchase.

Engels lifted a walkie-talkie to his mouth. "Stranger, come in."

"Stranger here, Colonel. Out."

"Standby. Set the howitzer's sights on our amigos in their fancy planes. Just in case."

"Yes, sir, Colonel," the voice crackled from the walkie-talkie. "Out."

"Still no word from Compton or Manders?" Engels asked Katterhagen.

Katterhagen cleared his throat, his eyes flickering under Engels's piercing stare. "No, sir. Should I send out a search patrol?"

"No. They're either on their way in," Engels said, disgusted, "or they're dead."

"Dead?"

"Bolan, you idiot," Engels rasped. "I'm really very displeased, Katterhagen, with how you've handled your duties here. You killed one old Indian, yet you didn't find any of the others. Any of whom can, and probably will, give the authorities a complete description of us and our operation. If we don't get safely into Mexico and to the coast, I'm holding you personally responsible.

"Not only that, but this madman, this Executioner, is still running wild out here somewhere. A madman you had a chance to get rid of from the beginning. But," Engels said, sighing heavily, "be all this as it may, we'll be gone in a matter of hours. Just the same, Katterhagen, there's going to be some changes after tonight."

Fear shadowed Katterhagen's features, his shoulders drawing back.

"Now, go get those punks out of those planes," Engels ordered, as the Bell 222 lowered from the sky, dust sheeting across the dirt runway. "Take them up near my quarters. And send someone to get that squaw. We're going to have a little going-away party, then we're getting the hell out of here."

As the landing skids touched earth, Engels strode away from Katterhagen to greet his PLO comrades.

Katterhagen held his ground for a moment, doubt and fear flooding dark shadows into his eyes.

FROM HIS HILLTOP vantage point, Bolan took in the scene along the runway through his twinned infrared binocs.

All the scum had gathered. And from what he could see, Bolan knew they weren't going to pull any punches from here on out.

Judging from the reception the new arrivals were given by Engels, as the outlaw operative clasped hands and embraced several of them, Bolan figured them to be the PLO slimeballs who'd come to purchase the massive arms shipment.

Men now slid the huge camo tarp off the cargo plane, and crates were hauled toward the freight plane by the dozen captives.

Thoroughly searching every nook, crevice and gully in the hills, Bolan counted only three sentries, two of whom manned the howitzer. The Executioner decided he would use the big gun to stage his all-out strike. With the 105 mm cannon and his RPG-7, he would lay waste every man and every piece of transportation on the runway.

The enemy numbers appeared to be packed into tight groups, as the preparations for departure were finalized. But, the night warrior knew, numbers were often deceptive. The hills could be alive with shadows ready to deal death in the blink of an eye.

And Bolan knew that every hard gun was on full alert.

Drugs. Arms. Scum.

Bolan had some hellfire, yeah, and he was going to rain it down on this Brigade, turn their Apocalypse on them. Whatever scheme Engels had devised, in collusion with the PLO scum, could not leave this desert. Or the carnage Engels had so far trailed would seem like some street gang fight in comparison to the death, destruction and human misery those crates of arms would wreak in the hands of international terrorists. Not to mention the heroin that would further poison the streets of America.

Bolan's first priority, though, was to round up and get the Navaho and Mexicans to safety. Somewhere. Anywhere. And that called for a silent and deadly penetration before the hard hit.

"I'm going with you. I will fight beside you," Young Eagle said, as he crouched next to Bolan. "I must help set my sister free. It is my right. She is all I have left."

Bolan admired the young man's bravery, impulsive and perhaps foolish as it was, but he couldn't bear to have Young Eagle's blood on his hands. Still, the Executioner could see that Young Eagle was bound and determined to make himself a pain in the ass, a pain that could well jeopardize the entire killing penetration.

Bolan decided he had to do something with Young Eagle, and perhaps, he allowed, the Navaho could serve some useful purpose after all.

"Okay, Young Eagle," Bolan grimly assented. "You want a piece of the action, here it is." Bolan handed Young Eagle the RPG-7. "Stuff your quiver with as many projectiles as you can. Set out along that ridge," he said, nodding toward the top of the hills to the east. "But only after me. You stay high; I go low. I'm taking out anything that moves in these hills, and then the two goons by that cannon."

Bolan rested a hard gaze on Young Eagle.

"Stay on that ridge above the cannon. Don't move. Don't do anything that would call attention to you. First thing I'm doing is going in after Golden Rainbow and the others. Once they're free, I'll move back to that howitzer. You stay on that hill until I get back." Bolan paused heavily, then added, "Your sister needs you alive."

Young Eagle smiled with a little too much enthusiasm for Bolan's liking.

"Gotcha," the Navaho said, reverting to slang he had put aside under Heart Sun's influence.

Lowering the NVD goggles over his eyes, Bolan strode out, climbing the rise that led toward the chain of hills. Crouched, the blacksuited nightscorcher darted from rock to rock, a silent wraith. With the silenced Beretta 93-R in his right hand, Big Thunder on his hip, the mini-Uzi slung around his right shoulder and spare clips for all three pieces packed inside his belt, Bolan shadowed up, then down along the hills.

The flares and floodlights clearly outlined the key members of Bolan's hit parade as they gathered near the wooden quarters, several hundred yards beyond the stalking phantom.

The ravine was about two hundred feet beyond the howitzer team, and Bolan judged the lowest and the safest drop point into the ravine to be about fifteen feet.

Combat senses on full alert, Bolan used the cover of boulders, dropped behind the rock, then down into narrow, shallow gullies cut by summer thunderstorms.

The inky blackness around Bolan was broken by moonlight.

There was an eerie stillness around him that the Executioner sensed, and recognized.

Death. Stalking.

Gravel crunching alerted Bolan to the unseen danger.

Out of nowhere, the shadow leaped up, stood above Bolan on the ridge.

Bolan swung, his Beretta tracking up at the shadow. But the gunman toppled, a soft grunt sounding before he plunged down the hill.

Bolan reached out and grabbed the dead man, stopping him from tumbling all the way to the bottom of the hill. The killing end of a broken arrow shaft seemed to grow out of the guy's temple. Looking up toward the high ground, Bolan found Young Eagle, who slowly waved his bow in a gesture of triumph.

"Hey, Benny."

Bolan froze.

This night was alive with headhunters, all right.

A head showed over the top of the next gully.

"Everything all right up there?"

"Everything is beautiful," the Man from Blood growled, and drilled a silenced 9 mm slug through the forehead that belonged to the voice.

In its own way, scum, Bolan thought, and moved on.

Checking the dead man, Bolan found a walkie-talkie. When the sentries didn't report in, and after what had gone down during his initial blitzkrieg, Bolan knew that Engels and his soldiers would be ready to open fire at the slightest sudden sound. But the Executioner was ready for this penetration to turn into a hard hit without warning. In fact, he counted on it.

He sensed that the night was alive with treachery.

Swifty, Bolan cut the gap to within thirty yards of the howitzer team, and he offered a silent thanks to nature for forming the rock outcrop that concealed the two-man team from the others down on the runway and near the quarters.

As he sighted down his Beretta on the two-man howitzer team, movement seemed to pick up near the quarters.

A car rolled toward Engels and his men.

When the vehicle was bathed for a second in the floodlights and light from the flares, Bolan instantly recognized it as Travers's cruiser.

There was no sign of a passenger.

Bolan cursed.

The dirty lawman had killed an innocent woman, and her unborn.

A pang of grief stabbed deep into the Executioner. Bolan would save Travers for last, if he could.

His rage fueled by the knowledge of Jamie's death, Bolan squeezed off a 3-round burst from his Beretta. The two dark lumps slumped down in death.

Angling down the hill toward the edge of the ravine, Bolan saw the captives hustled by Brigade soldiers toward the opening between the hills.

So far, his recon had paid off. His death strikes beyond the hardsite had reduced the numbers of the enemy considerably, and now the bulk of the enemy was just beyond the range of his gunsights.

The airstrip lights grew stronger as Bolan drew closer to the edge, and he removed his night vision goggles.

The Executioner slipped Little Lightning from around his shoulder, let the mini-Uzi fill his left hand.

ENGELS FELT an electrifying warmth spread through him as he noted the glint of blood lust in the eyes of Muhjan Azalbha.

The PLO man, Engels thought, was envisioning the terror he would strike into the hearts of his Western oppressors, the death and destruction he would rain down on his enemies if his demands were not met. Azalbha had already compiled a list of political enemies he intended to kidnap and hold for ransom. Azalbha's comrades in the Holy War would be freed from prison camps in Israel, and the West would hand over the Arab prisoners and millions of dollars to the PLO as ransom.

Engels knew that any man with a vision had to start somewhere, with some working capital. His PLO comrade was now receiving that working capital, in the form of AK-47s and RPG-7 rocket launchers, among high-powered explosives and grease guns. With Engels's help and guidance a new reign of terror was about to begin, with heavy and well-planned assaults already staged for hot spots across the Middle East and Africa.

The world would be gripped in fear, paralyzed by shock and horror at what Engels and the PLO would do. It was a glorious vision indeed, the outlaw operative thought, as he momentarily turned his attention toward the other PLO men.

Flare light flickered over the dark shapes of Azalbha's comrades. With the looks of hungry predators, they examined the rocket launchers and the MAC-10s.

"Where did you get all this, Colonel?" Azalbha inquired. His pearly-white teeth showed in a wide smile that cut the lines of his hawkish sunburned features.

"I had a man running arms for me down in Central America," Engels answered. "He was bringing the hardware in from East Germany through a group I dealt with on a cash-on-delivery basis. Unfortunately, my man was giving my merchandise away to some of his heroes down in El Salvador. At my expense completely, you understand. His piece of the action cost him all of the action. With his head."

"The swine!" Azalbha chuckled. "Greed," he mused. "I suppose it does get a good many of us."

"It sure does," Engels said, glancing at Salviche, who stood a dozen yards away from the mouth of the ravine, near the wooden quarters.

The druglord's right arm was wrapped inside a sling he'd made out of an undershirt. There was a large briefcase on the ground beside him.

Transaction money, Engels knew. Payoff cash. Dead man's paper.

Salviche, Bozzarelli and their limp guns, as the outlaw operative had repeatedly referred to them, were guarded by two soldiers with the red armband of the Apocalypse Brigade.

An oversize windbreaker covered Salviche, but still Engels detected the telltale bulge beneath the druglord's right armpit. Engels didn't believe Salviche was stupid enough to make some grandstand play—that would be suicide. The ex-CIA operative would hustle Salviche and the others to his quarters after dealing with the Arabs. Once inside, Engels would waste them all while the Arabs boarded the cargo plane.

A cargo plane bound for heaven, Engels thought with vicious sarcasm.

"*Bismillah irrahmam irrahim!*" Azalbha said, and put the AK-47 back into the crate. "In the name of Allah, the compassionate and the merciful, I believe there are great things ahead. For both of us. You have done well, my friend. We will fly together with the shipment. My men await us this very minute near Jordan."

"Good. Let me take care of some personal business over here, Muhjan," Engels said, "then we'll be on our way."

Azalbha nodded curtly. The PLO man and his comrades began walking toward the Bell 222.

Behind Engels the group of fifteen soldiers turned their attention toward Katterhagen as the German shoved a full-bodied, dark-skinned girl away from him.

Long strands of black hair fell over Golden Rainbow's face. Defiance showed in her dark eyes as she stared up at Engels.

Engels smiled, running his gaze up and down the length of her figure. "Golden Rainbow," he drawled. "Take her to my quarters."

A soldier took Golden Rainbow by the arm, led her away from the ravine.

Engels watched her leave, then turned grim-faced attention toward Salviche, took a step toward the druglord. Behind Engels, the Mexicans and Navaho were moved into the cave to bring out more crates. A pale glow of light wavered over them, then they vanished into the cave.

Travers stepped out of his cruiser, banged the door shut.

Glancing at the lawman, Engels growled, "What do you want now, Travers?"

"Money, mister. You still owe me."

"Sure. Sure. Be with you in a second," Engels answered abruptly, and ignored Travers.

Scowling, Travers thrust his hands on his hips.

"Throw me the briefcase, amigo. Time's up."

Salviche hesitated. Sweat sheened his brow, matted the hair to his neck.

Engels read the look of crazed fear in Salviche's eyes. He found himself enjoying the punk's discomfort, but an uneasy rumbling stirred in his belly all of a sudden. Warning hackles rose on the back of his neck. Engels pulled up a dozen feet short of Salviche.

A lump bobbed in Salviche's throat.

"Let's have it. Now, Salviche. I've got things to do."

Bending at the knees, Salviche stretched out a trembling hand for the briefcase.

"Me and you are going into my quarters. We'll have a little talk with the snakes there. About some snakes..."

Salviche galvanized himself into action, his hand streaking inside his jacket.

Travers's jaw went slack.

Engels and his soldiers froze for a heartbeat, unable, it seemed, to believe their eyes as the Magnum revolver was whipped from Salviche's jacket.

Salviche shoved one of his own men at the soldier next to him, the Brigade guard opening up with his HK-91.

"You goddamn crazy punk!" Engels roared, and dived as the Colt Python swung his way.

17

The murderous chaos that erupted below Bolan worked to his advantage. Obviously, the relationship between the druglords and Engels had soured, Bolan figured. But when cannibals worked together, greed and treachery often had a way of conspiring to turn the scum against each other.

Crouched behind a boulder atop the cave, Bolan stroked the mini-Uzi, raining death into that gorge. With short raking sweeps, the Executioner dropped ten soldiers in a flash.

The man whom Salviche threw toward the guard was ripped open by the Colt Commando bucking in that sentry's hands: the bullet-riddled body was slammed back into the mob of New Yorkers.

Engels belly-flopped to the ground, rolled, then jumped to his feet. As he launched himself over a boulder, Salviche's Python roared, 158-grain hollow-point projectiles blasting out chunks of stone that pelted into the back of the outlaw operative's head.

Katterhagen instantly flung himself back against the rock wall, scrambling desperately for the outcrop near the ravine's mouth.

Travers dropped to his stomach behind the cruiser. The Brigade gunners tumbled like bowling pins beneath the leaden rain washing over them from the dark lip of the gorge, flames stabbing through the blackness. Before death finally claimed the toppling hardmen, their assault rifles kept chattering in death-reflex action, bullets spewing out through winking muzzle-flashes. Ricochets, wild shots, tattooed the hood and doors of the cruiser. Glass shattered, cascading down on Travers.

Bolan took in the killzone with a glance, saw Azalbha and the rest of the PLO garbage sprinting for the Bell 222. The copter's blades slowly began spinning to life.

Then the night was suddenly split by a roaring fireball as the high explosive projectile erupted just behind the fleeing Arabs. Bodies cartwheeled through the air above the rolling smoke and flames.

Nosediving to the airstrip, Azalbha threw his arms over his head. His lips quivered in a silent prayer to Allah for deliverance. A dismembered leg thunked off the Arab's head.

Whirling, Bolan's gaze found the howitzer, following the line of yellow flame and rapidly thinning smoke. Even before he spotted Young Eagle—the Navaho was crouched beside the cannon—Bolan knew that the Indian had opted for the white man's high-tech warfare instead of the old ways of the bow.

Another HE projectile streaked away from the launcher.

The several surviving gunmen in the gorge scrambled for cover.

But they never made it.

The Executioner returned his hard-eyed battle mask toward the slaughter, a fresh 20-round clip in Little Lightning.

From the runway, Colt Commandos and HKs cut down the remaining New York muscle.

Salviche and Bozzarelli hurled themselves against the base of the quarters, slugs gouging out chunks of wood above their heads. Blood and gore from screaming men dancing death jigs splashed the wall.

Then the roof behind the druglords exploded into the sky on a geyser of flames, the front of the building beside them punched out by the tremendous concussion blasting from the HE missile.

Golden Rainbow and the Brigade member who held her captive were knocked to the ground.

Bolan cursed, well aware that Young Eagle hadn't seen his sister being hauled toward those quarters. At that moment, Bolan could only hope that Golden Rainbow was unharmed. He couldn't tell. The wall of the ravine blocked his view of the quarters.

Salviche raised his Colt Python. Teeth clenched, the druglord triggered a round that demolished the head of the Brigade soldier who was standing beside the Indian girl.

Two sentries, who'd been patrolling the perimeter to the south, came running up the airstrip. Their assault rifles held ready to join the firefight, they were outlined for a brief second by the floodlight.

In terrible pain, Salviche awkwardly fumbled with the Colt Python, fighting against time to reload. The explosion had distracted the sentries, and they appeared unaware that Salviche was even alive—until the druglord dropped them in their tracks with two head-shots.

Bolan heard the staccato chatter of an automatic weapon beneath him, saw the muzzle-flash from the mouth of the cave. The Navaho and the Mexicans were just inside the cave, he knew. Bolan had dropped two of the goons who were guarding the cave during his initial burst. The last soldier, gripped by panic, still triggered his weapon toward the group of spinning punks, whose bodies were chewed up further by his mindless assault even as they hit the ground dead.

Unleathering Big Thunder, Bolan leaped into the ravine. Landing softly just to the left of the cave, Bolan caught the soldier by surprise. The .44 flesh shredder bucked once, decapitated the machine pistol-wielding soldier at point-blank range.

Terror-stricken, the group of captives stared at the blacksuited, grim-faced warrior.

"You," the nightscorcher said to Running Elk. "When I tell you to get these people out of here, I'll cover you. Are there any others down there?"

Running Elk shook his head.

Bolan snatched up the MP-5 subgun, handed it to Running Elk. The Executioner's face was a sweat-slicked, stone-cold mask behind the wavering torch-light. Turning, pressed against the wall of rock, Bolan searched the shadows in the gorge, listening for any movement near him.

"When you hit it," Bolan told them, "hit it left. Keep to the far end, and get yourselves covered behind rock."

The chatter of semiauto-fire bounced off the walls of the ravine.

DEBRIS PLUNKED DOWN on Salviche. He flinched under the shower of wreckage as the smell of death, blood and smoke stung his nose, watered his eyes. Bozzarelli was stretched out behind him, right on his heels.

Salviche could almost feel the Italian quaking in fear, but he couldn't blame him for that. The blood-soaked bodies of their men were strewed all around them, a heaped tangle of arms and legs. Salviche, glancing at the wide, lifeless eyes that stared back at him as if in accusation, felt his own fear churning like a caldron in his bowels, the bile burning through his guts.

There was a lull in the firefight that made Salviche curious. He listened to the faint crackle of the flames leaping up from the leveled quarters beside him, felt the heat scorch his flesh. His heart pounded like a drum in ears still ringing from the deafening blasts. Looking out across the airstrip, he saw Engels's soldiers running toward the planes.

The cowards, he thought. They were fleeing for their lives. Then he realized they were leaving in his planes, and the Piper Cheyenne seemed to be his only hope of escape from the demon that had struck from out of the blackness and cut Engels's men down like a scythe through wheat.

Just who was he, Salviche wondered. What did he want? Why had he done this? Perhaps he was there to free the Navaho and the Mexicans. But why? And what did he care about them for?

It was clear to Salviche that whoever the stranger was, he wanted Engels dead. That meant Salviche had a chance to escape if Engels was the prime target, and for a moment the New Yorker was relieved that he hadn't gunned down the treacherous Engels. Hopefully the bastard in the ravine would take care of that for him.

Salviche looked at Golden Rainbow, who stirred in the dust near the end of the third quarters. The drug-lord told himself that he'd never make it to the plane without getting gunned down or blown up. And even if he did, he knew Engels's men would only kill him as soon as he set foot on that plane.

The squaw, he thought. She was his ticket out of there, even if he had to make it across the desert on foot. Whoever the gunman was who wanted Engels dead wouldn't blow Salviche away if he had a hostage, he reasoned.

This dude must have some decency after all, Salviche thought. He wanted to kill Engels, didn't he?

Colt Python in hand, Salviche crabbed on his knees and elbows toward Golden Rainbow.

"Where are you going?" Bozzarelli asked, his voice a hoarse whisper, the left side of his face coated with blood.

"I'm getting the hell out of here," Salviche rasped.

Crawling, Bozzarelli followed his drug-dealing companion, dragging a bloodied leg.

KATTERHAGEN BRACED HIMSELF against the wall of rock, the Colt Commando in his hand.

Dead men covered the ravine floor.

Tongues of fire lapped up the rubble that had been the first set of quarters.

It was insane, Katterhagen thought. What was the fighting for? Himself? The dream of world conquest? Engels?

He owed Engels nothing.

The German saw the others running toward the planes, and cursed them. He cursed Azalbha as the Arab, too, raced for his helicopter. They were deserting, turning tail and running because the scene had gotten a little too hot, because one man had sent their dreams crumbling down around them. Hell, they could at least pin Bolan down while he made his way out of there, Katterhagen thought bitterly.

The operation was finished, he knew, and he would be dead if the hellstormer who was called the Executioner had anything to say about it.

Engels was directly across the ravine from Katterhagen. The German saw his leader pointing toward the cave, indicating Bolan's position. What did Engels

expect him to do? Walk down the middle of the gorge
and start blasting away? There was no chance Katterhagen could get off a clean shot at Bolan as long as he
stayed inside the cave.

Engels's hand snaked out, hauling in an HK-91.

The cruiser was less than a dozen yards away from
Katterhagen. Reaching cover behind the bullet-
ravaged cruiser would be his first step to escape. Then
he'd make a break for one of the aircraft or a jeep.

It was now or never, he decided.

Katterhagen shoved himself off the wall, and
bolted. He zigzagged the first few steps, then hit the
ground, rolling.

BOLAN LEVELED the stainless-steel hand cannon to
trigger a round at Katterhagen, but a tide of .308
tumblers washed over the mouth of the cave, forcing
him back into cover. Slugs sizzled past Bolan's face,
whizzed by his ears before pounding into rock, spraying chunks of stone into his face.

Katterhagen finished his sprint, bounded up onto
the cruiser's hood and dived behind the car.

Bolan knew Engels had secured cover behind the
boulder cluster, but he hadn't seen the outlaw operative take the piece of hardware.

More hot lead poured over Bolan's position. He
couldn't afford to get pinned down—a well-tossed
grenade, or an HE projectile would bring tons of rock
down on him and the others, sealing them in an
earthen tomb.

Crouching low, Bolan waited for the lull in the heavy fire. When it came, he peered around the edge, saw Engels break for the wreckage.

Bolan leaned out of the cave, mini-Uzi blazing, but Engels was already behind the barrier of rubble.

"Is there another way out of this ravine?" Bolan asked, retreating back into the cave.

"There's a gully toward the end. It leads to the top." Running Elk answered.

"Okay. Move it out!" Bola rasped, and cut Little Lightning loose on the cruiser, pinning down Travers and Katterhagen while the Navaho and Mexicans broke from out of the cave.

THE BULLET IN BOZZARELLI'S THIGH shot a searing pain through his whole body. Limping, the Italian druglord hugged the wall of Engels's quarters, fearful of exposing himself to any gunfire. He lagged several dozen steps behind Salviche and the Indian girl.

Then Bozzarelli heard the chatter of an Uzi behind him. Turning, he saw Engels darting out of the ravine.

"Armando!" Bozzarelli yelled as Engels swung his assault rifle toward them.

Salviche whirled, thundering three quick rounds toward Engels.

Stumbling, Engels plunged into the wreckage. Jumping to his feet, he triggered the HK-91. Slugs, muzzle-flash parted the tendrils of smoke from the flames consuming the rubble beside Engels.

Weaponless, Bozzarelli slammed himself into the wall, away from the deadly line of fire. Lunging for the door, he felt a .308 slug tear his arm. Spinning, the Italian druglord crashed through the door.

Gunfire, shouting and cursing became a shattered roar inside Bozzarelli's head. Mind-numbing agony paralyzed him for a long moment. His breathing was loud and sharp in his ears as he crawled several feet into the quarters, praying that Engels would pass him by in his murderous pursuit of Salviche.

The darkness around Bozzarelli became impenetrable.

Something made a scratching sound near his face, and Bozzarelli froze, remembering what had taken place, what he'd seen that afternoon in the room. He sensed movement all around him, coming at him from the blackness, from across the floor, drawn to him as if he were a magnet.

A knifelike pain suddenly stabbed into his legs, and kept knifing into his flesh like razored pincers.

Finally the sound of rattlers broke through his state of shock and horror.

Bozzarelli heard a scream form in his mind, but the scream never reached his lips.

He felt the fangs spear into his cheeks, ripping the flesh off his face.

The scream broke from his throat, a banshee shriek of stark and brutal terror.

At that moment Engels swung into the doorway, stood, as if mesmerized by what he saw, the assault rifle sweeping up in his hands.

The screams ended.

The stench of excrement wafted up to the outlaw operative's nose.

Except for the generator-powered floodlights there would have been total darkness around Engels. Still, enought light outlined the fat-bodied shapes of his serpents, his pets slithering around the torn and bloodied body of the Italian druglord.

A druglord he had created and brought to power many years ago.

A punk that he was glad was dead.

Shock waves had knocked the glass cages to the floor. The fierce firefight had violently agitated the dozen rattlesnakes, and they were still striking the dead Bozzarelli.

Footfalls sounded. Engels spun, his HK-91 tracking toward Travers and Katterhagen.

Breathless, the two men pulled up beside Engels. Both men looked through the doorway, their expressions taut.

"Jesus," Travers breathed.

"Why didn't you cover me?" Engels growled at Katterhagen.

"What the hell was I supposed to do?" Katterhagen shot back. "There was no way I could've gotten him from that angle back there. No way."

Engels looked away from Katterhagen in disgust. He saw the Bell 222 preparing to lift off, then heard the turbojet engines of the Piper Cheyenne scream to life. Dust swirled across the runway, covering the dead Arabs.

Turning, Engels found no sign of Salviche and Golden Rainbow. He cursed. Everything had blown up in his face, his dream shattered by a blacksuited demon named Mack Bolan.

"Where did Bolan go?" Engels demanded.

"He covered for the others," Katterhagen answered, "while they ran out of the cave."

"He left the ravine?"

"I didn't see him," Katterhagen said.

"What do you mean, you didn't see him?" Engels snapped.

"Only thing I can figure is that he climbed the gully out of there."

"The howitzer," Engels muttered. "That gun's turned on the planes."

"With our guys in them," Katterhagen said.

"What if they're waiting for us?" Travers asked.

Engels's lips curled over his teeth. "What's with this 'us' crap, Travers? Does it look like they're waiting for us? Shit, no! Those loyal soldiers of mine are cutting out."

Engels wheeled, searching the darkness to the south. "Right now, I'm going after that bastard, Salviche. I want to look him right in the eye when I blow him away."

"The planes, Colonel," Katterhagen said. "They might just be waiting for us, you think?"

"Forget them," Engels growled. "They'll all be history in about one minute, count on it. And you'd better believe Bolan's going to be coming after us next. Now, the three of us stand a good chance of beating him out there on the desert, instead of standing around here and playing his game, while he picks us off in the dark. It sure looks like I couldn't count on you and your handpicked buddies, Katterhagen, to do the job of nailing this bastard. Now, I've got to do it myself." Engels looked at Travers, hard-eyed. "If you're coming along, throw that piece away; I trust you like I've got eyes in the back of my head."

Travers seemed set to protest, but unholstered the .44 Magnum, and tossed it aside.

"Now, if there's anything here when we get back, then we'll salvage what we can and get out of here." Engels held his icy gaze on both men for another moment. "That is, *if* we're still alive."

SILENTY BOLAN JUMPED DOWN beside Young Eagle, plucked the rocket launcher out of his hands.

Young Eagle appeared stunned, unaware that the Navaho and Mexicans had gathered behind him.

If they'd been anyplace else, Bolan thought, he might have decked Young Eagle. But there wasn't a second to waste. The aircraft on the runway was ready to depart from the killzone.

This desert war was not over yet.

"You don't listen well at all, Young Eagle," Bolan growled.

"I could've killed her," Young Eagle murmured in disbelief, a haunted look of shame in his eyes. "I didn't see her...I didn't know...I was so..."

"Look with your eyes and not your heart and those things won't happen," Bolan said.

"One of them took her," Young Eagle informed Bolan, snapping himself out of his brooding and self-pity, pointing south. "I saw Engels and two others follow him. They ran off into the night. Like the cowards they are. They're gone."

Bolan lined up the RPG's sights on the Bell 222 as the copter climbed out of the beam of light. The distance was a little more than six hundred yards. One shot was all Bolan would get.

The launcher shuddered, and the rocket streaked away into the night.

One shot was all Bolan needed.

A fiery ball mushroomed in the dark sky, blazing over the runway.

As the flaming wreckage plummeted to the airstrip, Bolan set the launcher down to man the recoilless cannon.

"Give me a hand here," he ordered over his shoulder to the man behind him.

Every living soul in the area stopped cold in their tracks.

Engels, Travers and Katterhagen saw the brilliant flash, heard the powerful explosion that blew the Bell 222 out of the sky.

The Piper Cheyenne began to roll.

The mighty cannon boomed from the hills.

Rolling thunder.

The 105 mm artillery shell impacted into the fuselage, and the turbojet was obliterated, swept off the runway by an awesome, ear-shattering detonation.

Another night-splitting peal several seconds later, and the other turbojet exploded into scraps of flying metal, the explosion hurling warped sheets off the runway on screaming balls of fire as if they were nothing more than garbage can lids lost in the sucking maw of a hurricane.

THE NAVAHOS AND MEXICANS helped Bolan swing the field gun around on its turntable.

A Mexican loaded a shell into the breech, and Bolan carefully realigned the sights to target the cargo plane.

They covered their ears, all eyes turned in the direction of the stationary target.

The shell cannoned from the muzzle, left a deafening peal of roaring sound like a thunderclap in its wake. And the artillery projectile exploded into the hull, the earthshaking blast and the shell frag pattern pulping the freight plane.

But Bolan wasn't finished.

Far from it.

Bolan addressed the group. "I'm going after the men who took Golden Rainbow. Don't anyone follow me; you'll only get in the way," he said, glancing at Young Eagle. "They're all dead except for those four men. You've got nothing to fear now. Get back to your people."

Bolan made to leave, but Running Elk called out. "I don't know who you are, or why you did this, but I thank you. For all of us. We owe you our lives. They were going to kill us."

Bolan looked at Running Elk. "Just go on with your lives, and stay strong. That'll be thanks enough."

Quickly, Bolan made his way back to the ravine with the rocket launcher in his hand. There he loaded the RPG-7 with a projectile from one of the full crates. With cold, methodical precision, Bolan laid waste the rest of the enemy's hardsite.

A projectile sealed the mouth of the cave.

Three explosions, each following the other within seconds, turned the three jeeps into useless scrap metal, vaporized rubber.

Another rocket blew the rest of the quarters into the sky.

Shards of wood, chunks of twisted metal, jagged slabs of granite and bits of human and snake flesh rained down on the desert.

Rolling thunder.

Fiery rain.

From the flaming airstrip, walls of fire crackling behind him, the nightscorcher triggered one last rocket that blew the crates of weapons in the ravine off the face of the earth.

Forever.

Then the night warrior left that hellzone.

To take his war out into the desert.

It became personal now.

Cold-blooded.

Man on man.

The night swallowed up the Executioner in its beckoning maw.

Another innocent life was balanced on the threshold of eternity.

18

Dawn streaked across the horizon, shedding a dirty gray light over the broken, barren land.

The night warrior now became the hunter.

A headhunter.

From a chain of jagged ridges beyond the southern hills of the flaming hardsite, and several hours before the break of the new day, Bolan had spotted the black shapes of his quarry. Through his light-gathering night lenses, he had seen them moving like phantoms across the desert.

Stalking them by jeep, Bolan knew, would have alerted them to his position. Instead, the Executioner opted to track them, hunt them down on foot. He had elected to don a uniform he'd stripped from a dead Brigade soldier, instead of moving across the desolate land in combat blacksuit. The blacksuit would have made him stand out like a wart on a witch's nose under the glare of oncoming daylight.

Since fleeing the ruins of their compound and the fiery end of their master scheme to combine forces with the PLO and begin massive terrorist strikes in the Middle East, the traitorous trio of Engels, Travers and

Katterhagen had used the cover of night, opened up a good two and a half miles between themselves and their invisible stalker.

Keeping to the high ground, Bolan now moved in behind their position down in the valley. They were still about a mile away, out of his gunsights.

Dropping down into a prone position along the ridge of a high hill, Bolan marked their progress through his field glasses.

Engels led the way. It became quickly apparent to Bolan that the Apocalypse Brigade leader was heading south. Frequently, Engels stopped and scoured the hills around them, searching the ground in front of him, pointing. They moved swiftly but cautiously though arroyos, hidden for long stretches from Bolan. When visible, they skirted the base of the hills, using the cover of boulders whenever possible.

There was no sign of Golden Rainbow. Reviewing the action that had started the firefight, and recalling that he'd seen no sign of the druglords after all hell had broken loose, Bolan believed one of them had the Indian girl.

She was the one whom Engels wanted.

With a .444 Marlin rifle, which he'd secured from the back of the Jimmy before abandoning the vehicle, and Big Thunder riding on his hip, Bolan set out. He intended to close the gap from behind the cannibals, and drop them where they stood.

GOLDEN RAINBOW STUMBLED, cried out in pain as Salviche dragged her for several steps along the canyon floor. Then, cursing her viciously, he jerked the Navaho girl to her feet.

But Salviche cursed himself as much as he did the girl. She'd cost him precious time with her resistance. Once she'd even broken free of his grasp, and run. The ugly, dark welts around her mouth and the bruise beneath her left eye were the results of his rage over his own idea to bring her along as a hostage.

"C'mon, get up, damn you, squaw!" he snarled, twisting her arm, hauling her along beside him.

Salviche saw the charred wreckage, but in his haste and fear he didn't think twice about the downed copters.

With a wild look in his eyes, the New York drug king stared up at the towering rock walls.

Salviche heard his empty belly rumble with hunger. His arms and legs seemed like deadweight in his exhaustion. His lips were cracked and burning, and his throat and mouth felt as if they'd been sandpapered raw. Every step came only with a concentrated effort. And the pain in his broken hand grew worse; the throbbing seemed to have turned the blood in his arm into fire.

Dried sweat had plastered strands of hair across Golden Rainbow's face, and her dark eyes blazed with anger and defiance.

Salviche stopped, listened. Silently he swore that he heard a noise along the rim of the canyon. The flanking walls appeared to close in on him. His heart pounded like a jackhammer in his chest. The air rasped out of his flared nostrils.

Salviche let go of Golden Rainbow, brandished the .357 Colt Python.

Someone was up there on the rim, he was certain.

With his gun hand, Salviche backhanded Golden Rainbow to the ground.

"Run and I'll kill you right here, understand?"

"Freeze, asshole."

Whirling, Salviche found the shadow that stood in the mouth of the ravine ahead of him.

A long burst of HK-91 fire roared, .308 tumblers stitching the druglord's chest and stomach, spinning Salviche around, hammering him into the ground. The HK's chattering racket bounced off the canyon walls, the echo lingering for a long moment.

Katterhagen and Travers strode up toward the fallen pusher from the north end of the canyon.

Engels joined the two men, all three now standing over the bullet-riddled body.

Blood trickled from Salviche's mouth. Even in his dying moment, he injected hatred into his eyes. Coughing, he cracked open his lips, struggled to speak.

Salviche's head lolled to the side.

"You were always just a punk, Salviche," Engels said. "You died a punk's death."

A smile started to stretch Katterhagen's lips, then his head exploded.

Blood and gore splattered Engels's clothes.

The rifle's explosive peal washed through the gorge.

Travers dived behind a boulder.

As Katterhagen's headless body toppled, Engels seized Golden Rainbow, threw her into the gully, dropped down on top of her.

Total silence.

Engels felt his fear mount as the seconds dragged.

"Looks like you've been busy here, Bolan!" Engels shouted. "I know it's the squaw you want, but I got her first. You want her, you come down here and get her. Nice and peaceful. With your hands in the air. You've got ten minutes, Bolan, you hear me? Ten minutes to show your bloody ass or I'll throw this squaw to the snakes. You ruined me, bastard! Payback time. An eye for an eye."

Travers belly-crawled along the base of the wall.

"Hey, bastard," Engels called again. "I know you won't let the squaw die. Yeah, that's the problem with you. You've got a soft spot in your heart for all the wrong people. You could've made it in the world, Bolan, but you chose to fight for something that isn't worth dying for. You're stupid, Bolan. You've got guts, but you're stupid. Hey, you think anybody really gives a damn about what you're doing? Well, I'm willing to find out just how much this Indian bitch means to you. You hear me, Bolan? She's one dead squaw, crusader. You've got nine minutes now."

Assault rifle in hand, Engels stood, hauled Golden Rainbow to her feet.

BOLAN HEARD, ALL RIGHT. His guts knotted up with rage.

The taunting voice of the renegade seemed to echo through the early morning chill around Bolan.

As soon as he'd dropped Katterhagen with a decapitating shot from the Marlin, Bolan had moved out from his hilltop kill point just north of the canyon.

Quickly, the Executioner climbed up the trail that led to the high ground. He held the .44 AutoMag in his right hand, his eyes fixed on the ridge of jagged rocks above him. He had two hundred yards beyond that ridge, he figured, until he closed in on the mesa where Engels would make his last stand.

The uphill going was treacherous and slower than Bolan wanted. The path was littered with rocks and in some places huge boulders blocked his way.

Topping the trail, chancing exposure to unseen gunfire from out of the murky light, Bolan leaped over several boulders, made his way along the rim. Silently he drew nearer to the ledge that, if he remembered correctly from the night before, overlooked the fissure. Which was alive with venomous serpents.

"Yeah, you been real busy, I can see, bastard!" Bolan heard Engels yell. The Executioner strained his ears to pinpoint the renegade's position.

Just over the next rise, he knew.

A scream.

The sound of a palm cracking like a whip over flesh.

"No!"

Golden Rainbow.

"Bolan! Bolan!"

The man was insane with rage and fear, the Executioner judged from the sound of his voice, a voice that sounded more animal than human.

"Two minutes, Bolan! Shut up, bitch."

Bolan topped the next rise. He dropped down behind a line of rocks, the stainless-steel hand cannon swinging up in his fist.

But Bolan didn't, couldn't fire.

Engels stood along the edge of the crevice, looking up at Bolan. The outlaw was using Golden Rainbow as a human shield. Captor and hostage were only inches from the brink.

"I figured you'd try that," Engels said, a cold smile over his lips. "I've had a couple months more than you to get to know this desert."

"Let the girl go, Engels." Bolan gestured with the AutoMag. "It's just you and me now."

Engels crouched low behind the girl, keeping himself almost completely concealed from Bolan. Captor and captive stood at an angle, twenty-five feet away from the ice-eyed man on the ledge.

At the moment, Bolan knew he couldn't risk firing a shot, fearful that the girl would be shoved or dropped into the snake pit.

A strange light shone in Engels's eyes. Dry laughter cracked from his throat.

"You can't get a shot off from there, right?" Engels goaded. "You shoot me, you know she goes right in. Looks like we've got ourselves a standoff, but we can change that, Mr. Executioner. You drop the gun and come down here and I'll let the squaw go. Your life for hers. Fair enough, huh?''

Engels waited.

"Drop it, bastard!" he snarled. "Now."

"Move away from the edge a few steps, Engels. First," Bolan said, his voice icy. "I need some assurance she's going to go free. Then you can have me."

Engels hesitated. "All right," he conceded. He took a step back, the HK-91 angling toward Bolan.

Slowly, the Executioner stood.

"The gun, Bolan, drop it!"

Bolan blazed into action. Big Thunder roared, a 240-gram slug blowing off the hand that held the assault rifle.

Bolan sprang away from the ledge.

Engels spun, screamed, crunched to the ground. Golden Rainbow lost her balance, teetered on the lip of the crevice.

Bolan launched himself off the edge, sweeping past Golden Rainbow, his arm slamming into her chest. The impact pounded Golden Rainbow to the ground.

Bolan hit the mesa, rolled, jumped to his feet.

Engels lunged for the assault rifle, blood jetting from the stump where his hand had been.

Bolan reached for Engels as an arrow drilled into the back of the outlaw operative's thigh.

Young Eagle had exploded back into Bolan's war.

Another arrow followed the first in a lightning whish, spearing into the back of Engels's knee. The renegade cried out in pain.

Bolan glimpsed Young Eagle out of the corner of his eye. The Navaho was kneeling along the far east edge of the mesa.

Then the Executioner turned his wrath on Engels. Bolan grabbed a handful of Engels's shirt, the other hand hooking inside the renegade's belt. With rage-powered might, the Executioner lifted Engels off the ground, high above his head.

"Nooo!" Engels pleaded.

Bolan hurled Engels into the pit.

Engels's body bounced down the side of the wall. Jutting, knifelike rocks shredded his clothes to bloodied tatters. The Company man gone bad hit bottom with a bone-snapping thud.

But Engels survived the fall.

Bolan straightened to his full height, his chest heaving for a second from the sudden exertion. He felt the terrible rage slowly ebb, turn into a cold hardness.

Cries of pain and horror shrilled up from the pit.

Her punished features tight with fear, Golden Rainbow stared up at Bolan.

"You all right," Bolan quietly asked her.

She nodded.

Bolan helped her to stand.

As Young Eagle ran toward them, Bolan growled, "How come you won't listen to anybody?"

Golden Rainbow and Young Eagle embraced, seemed purposefully oblivious to anything around them during their moment of reunion.

Bolan shook his head, angry with Young Eagle for interfering again.

"Sister, sister, you're safe. We can go home."

Bolan took a step toward his AutoMag.

"Hold it right there, Sarge."

Bolan froze, several feet from his piece.

Golden Rainbow and Young Eagle turned their heads, fear shadowing their faces.

Travers, his face swollen and lopsided from his brawl with Bolan, moved away from the gully. Katterhagen's Colt Commando was in his hands, trained, steady as rock, on Bolan.

"You've just done me a big favor," Travers drawled, stepping over the body of Compton, moving toward the lip of the fissure. There, he glanced down into the pit.

The thrashing, the screaming had stopped.

"I've just bagged me the biggest killer this country's ever seen," the lawman went on. "A fugitive wanted by every law enforcement agency across the world, I hear."

Bolan just looked at Travers, his gaze stone cold.

"Isn't that right, Bolan?" Travers asked. "You see, the way I figure it, you came out here to New Mexico and decided to once more take the law into your hands. Only this time, you got nailed. You've killed how many men? A thousand? Two, three thousand during this lone crusade of yours since Nam? Hell, I'm looking at maybe a hundred dead men out here now. That's an awful lot of first-degree murder counts, the way I'm seeing things. Not only that, I tried to stop you back in town. Remember? They call what you did back there fleeing the scene of a crime, a felony, to be specific. Tack on another charge of assaulting a police officer with intent to commit murder.''

A leaden silence dropped over the mesa.

Hatred crept into the lawman's stare.

''It's all over, Bolan,'' Travers sneered. ''The crusade stops here. I'll cut you down, then those two with Engels's piece. The Feds'll be swarming all over this desert before too long now. And you know what they'll find?'' Travers paused heavily. ''One gutsy bitch of a lawman who went after Mack the Executioner Bolan on his own. And nailed his murdering ass after one long heroic kill hunt. That's what the papers will read. And who will be around to deny it?''

Travers shrugged, chuckled.

A lone gunshot broke the early morning stillness.

Cloth and flesh sheared away from Travers's arm on a spray of blood.

Bolan jolted his head sideways, found Jamie standing at the top of the gully.

The Colt Python bucked in her two-fisted grip. A 158-grain hollowpoint slug tunneled through Travers's stomach, doubling him over, punching him around, a look of agony and sheer amazement on his face.

The lawman appeared to meet Jamie's gaze for a split second before the Colt Python roared for a third and final time. The round blasted into Travers's arm, kicked him over the edge.

The big gun fell from Jamie's hands. She looked at Bolan, and collapsed as he moved toward her.

Bolan knelt beside the woman, found her pulse, weak, but it was there. Dust was glued to her face by dried sweat; her hair fell, a tangled mane across her features.

"Jamie?"

Her eyelids fluttered open. "God…I'm so thirsty," she said, her voice hoarse and cracking.

Golden Rainbow and Young Eagle stood behind Bolan.

"Take it easy, lady," Bolan told her. "You're going to be all right."

"The baby?"

"Yeah, the baby, too."

"Some hero, wasn't he?" She forced a bitter smile. "He was one of them. He might as well have killed his own son. He was worse than them…because he wore a badge."

Bolan clenched his jaw. She was right. For some reason it always seemed worse when someone who wore a uniform, who was supposed to uphold law and justice, went bad.

Bolan studied the woman. She was dehydrated, exhausted and she needed medical attention fast, as much for herself as for the unborn child she carried. But she was a fighter, a survivor, Bolan knew. She would carry the scars of this desert battle for the rest of her life, but the suffering she'd endured would leave her stronger than before, when she was able to look back on it.

"Kent always tried to prove he was half the man his father was. I wonder... I wonder how Kent would've felt now if... if..."

She swallowed painfully. Anguish showed in her haunted stare.

Bolan looked away from her, up at the sky. His own grief cut deep into his war-torn soul.

Young Eagle held his sister close to him.

The light of dawn broke over the plateau.

Bolan wondered about Heart Sun. He remembered the chieftain's words, the vision he'd seen. Bolan heard the Navaho's voice, so clear and strong in his mind that Heart Sun's words seemed to call out to Bolan from somewhere above the mesa.

Wind soughed behind the tableau of survivors. Dust stirred around the dead.

Had Heart Sun's prophecy been confined to this stretch of blood-drenched desert, Bolan wondered.

Or was the worst yet to come?

Mack Bolan didn't need the answer to that.

He knew.

War Everlasting.

Gently, Bolan scooped Jamie up in his arms.

High above the mesa, a black crow spread its wings, soared silent as death across the desert sky.